Angela Huth has written seven novels, two collections of short
stories, a work of non-fiction and a book for children as well as
plays for television, radio and the stage. She is also a
broadcaster, critic and occasional journalist. She lives with her
husband, a university don, in Oxford, and has two daughters.

Invitation to the Married Life

"A first class writer ... she shows off her talents for comedy and
pathos to equally telling effect"

Sunday Telegraph

"A superbly domestic novel ... lovingly perceptive. Any reader
of Jane Austen will take to this exploration of the married state
instantly, for it is the kind of thing Jane Austen
might well have written if she had got married and amused her
readers with the trials and rewards she found in that state"

Evening Standard

Land Girls

"Angela Huth's riveting novel ... is evocative and entertaining"

Mail on Sunday

"It had me in its grip and I couldn't rest until the final page ... It
is satisfying and rare to read a book whose characters are dealt
the fates we feel they deserve ... A beautifully spun tale that
absorbs without the need to address 'issues'"

Literary Review

Nowhere Girl

ANGELA HUTH

An *Abacus* Book

First published in Great Britain by Collins, 1970
This edition published by Abacus, 1995

A CIP catalogue record for this book
is available from the British Library.

ISBN 0 349 10630 4

Printed and bound in Great Britain by Clays Ltd, St. Ives plc

Abacus
A Division of
Little, Brown and Company (UK)
Brettenham House
Lancaster Place
London WC2E 7EN

For Various People

Chapter One

My first husband, Richard Storm, was buried on a hot August day in the suburbs of London. When the funeral was over, a dozen of us, relations and friends, drove away in a procession of big black cars. Their seats had been built to force passengers into upright positions of respect. We sat uncomfortably and no-one spoke a word.

Richard's parents lived in a dark flat near Hyde Park. At their invitation we joined them there to re-form the funeral group we had made round the coffin, only this time it was round a table laid with fishpaste sandwiches. We drank sweet sherry and talked in cheerless tones appropriate to the occasion.

I left at four, the first to leave, and walked into the park. It was very hot, oppressively hot. The trees were quite still, like trees under snow. People walked slowly, or slept on the grass, careless of their appearance, legs apart, hands straggling over faces, like people on a beach. The sherry still tasted horrible in my mouth, and the skirt of my black dress clung damply to my legs.

There was no hurry. There was nothing to hurry for, and it was too thundery to hurry.

I sat on a bench. It was already half-occupied by two old women. They sat alert, on the very edge of the bench, as if they were about to move, but were waiting for some signal. In a way, they resembled some of the old people who had been at the funeral, except they were poorer. The one farthest from me was shrivelled into a bow shape, scraggy and grey. Grey skin, grey eyes, black coat faded almost to grey. She stared straight ahead and let the ugly knots of her hands lie dead in her lap.

The one nearest to me looked healthier, altogether sprightlier. She too had a black coat, but a poppy left over from some long past Poppy Day stuck in the brim of her hat.

She turned to me and said:

'You can hear the buses from here, can't you? That's nice.'

I listened. I could hear the rumble of buses.

'So you can,' I said.

'That's what I like about it here. You can sit down and listen to the noise, and yet you're in a nice bit of green.' She looked at the prickly hedge opposite our bench, the rim of scorched grass by the path, the litter-bin, and a motionless tree. 'Oh no,' she went on, 'I've nothing to grumble about now, have I? I never liked the quietness of the old days, you know. What I like is a supermarket on a Saturday morning. Or those demonstrations in Trafalgar Square. As a matter of fact, I was at one of those not long ago. I'm not quite sure what it was all about, to be honest, but there I was shouting away with the rest of them, and one of those policemen nearly took me away in a van. "Not on your life, officer," I said to him. "There's no law against innocent shouting. Besides, I'm enjoying myself." And his hands just fell away from me.'

She smiled. Her voice was quiet, but not so quiet as Mrs Storm's had been. Mrs Storm was Richard's mother. My presence at his funeral had embarrassed her. She had nodded to me in the church, and looked confused. Later, in the hot brown room, sickly with the smell of nervous sweat, she shook my hand and said:

8

'Oh, Clare, how nice to have the chance to see you again.' Then she coughed, and blushed a deep yellow-pink, realising that was not what she had meant.

She wore a musquash coat. All the women seemed to be in musquash coats, in spite of the heat. A mournful fur. They held their sherry in damp hands that left fingerprints on their glasses. They were hungry for the fishpaste sandwiches which Mrs Storm handed round. A gathering of mustard and cress had caught up in the short grey hairs on her top lip. She must have been conscious of them, because when I went to say good-bye her small mauve tongue darted to the corners of her mouth, and she bumped nervously against her husband like a pigeon on a high ledge.

The old woman on the bench was talking again.

'My sister, now,' she was saying, 'my sister is quite different from me. She doesn't agree with me at all.' She nudged the other old woman who turned reluctantly towards me. An empty face. A portrait whose oil paint has been scraped from it, leaving nothing but a faint drawing beneath. She blinked, so slowly that when her lids lowered I had a feeling that they wouldn't rise again.

'My sister always was the quiet one. Her name's Edith. Edith Smith. She never married, you see.' With her right hand Edith Smith's sister rubbed at the rings on the third and fourth fingers of her left hand. Next to her wedding ring she wore a small, dark ruby ring set in silver. On her third finger, a round, pearly blue star-sapphire. The fine rays of its star glinted in the sun. 'And my name is Ethel Fox. Mrs Henry Fox, though Henry died fourteen years ago.' Edith Smith blinked slowly again, in confirmation of all this.

'It's one of Edith's days in London,' Mrs Fox went on.

'She lives in the Gulliver Old People's Home in Herne Bay, and she's allowed up twice a year. Usually, we have a good time. But it's been rather heavy to-day, and Edith's feet are aching.' One of Edith's shiny black walking shoes twitched almost imperceptibly. 'Still, we had a nice lunch in Lyons, then bought some embroidery silks in Barkers. – Edith's good with her hands,' she added.

We sat in silence for a while. The air was still and lifeless, like it sometimes is before an August storm. The sky was piling up with sour green clouds. Mrs Fox was looking at them.

'It's rather far to go back to my flat,' she said, 'all the way to Earl's Court. And anyway, what can two people like us do just sitting in a room?' At that moment two large drops of rain broke on the path by our feet. Mrs Fox brightened.

'It's coming on to rain,' she said. 'Edith, it's coming on to rain. For myself, I don't mind being caught in a shower because I never catch colds. But it's Edith we must think of. Edith, come along.'

The two old women stood up. Mrs Fox took her sister's arm.

'Where do you think we should go?' she asked. Standing, she held herself very straight. Beside her, Edith Smith sagged, a crumpled piece of indeterminate grey, and yet she lacked that quality of inconspicuousness that makes some people stand out in a crowd.

'You could come back with me,' I said.

'That's the answer,' said Mrs Fox. 'We'll come back with you.'

We hurried along, the three of us, our heels rattling out-of-step on the pavements, past the Albert Hall, down the Exhibition Road. The rain thumped down slowly but spitefully. We concentrated on speed. At the funeral, the coffin bearers had concentrated on careful slowness. They were very good at it, and didn't joggle the coffin on their shoulders. Their lips were sucked in with concentration so that their mouths were thin pencil lines. At the church they all took off their top hats with one gesture, like chorus men in a variety show.

We reached the house – small, trim, pretty, in a narrow cobbled mews. Geraniums in the window boxes flared scarlet against the white paint. The gilt door-knocker and knob were of matching intricate design.

'I've always wondered what sort of people lived in these sort of houses,' said Mrs Fox, as I opened the door.

In the sitting-room Edith Smith at once fell back on to the sofa, tired. Her weight barely made an impact on the fat cushions. Mrs Fox stared curiously at a picture of Richard above the fireplace. A crayon drawing he had done in Salisbury as a present for our first wedding anniversary. He was dressed in naval uniform, sharp, antiseptic – attractive, I had thought, at seventeen. A mild but distant face. Certainly he didn't look the sort of man who would marry a girl twenty years younger than himself, treat her like a spoilt child for a couple of years, then desert her for a middle-aged woman called Matilda he met one leave in Barcelona. Our divorce had been very easy. Plain desertion. And Richard had remained friendly. He sent me cards on my birthday and at Christmas, and encouraged Matilda to send me boxes of liqueur-filled chocolates.

'That your husband?' Mrs Fox asked.

'It was, but he died. That's my husband now.' I pointed to a photograph of Jonathan in a silver frame. A kind but weak face, a little fleshy under the re-touched eyes, the mouth too full and high for its width.

'Oh, I see.' She fingered the frame. 'Is he musical?'

'Not particularly. He likes Strauss.'

'I thought he might be. He's got a musical face. But then Henry looked musical, and he couldn't tell Haydn from Mozart. So you never can tell.' She walked over to the record player. 'Could we put something on?'

'Strauss?'

'Oh no, not in this rain. Have you anything by the Beatles?'

I put on a record.

'"Lucy in the Sky,"' said Mrs Fox. 'I'd like Edith to hear that.' She turned up the volume herself and smiled. Edith Smith shut her eyes. I went to get the tea.

The time the sisters took to eat seemed to go very slowly. Mrs Fox and I nodded and smiled to one another as the biscuits were passed to and fro. Edith appeared as ex-communicated as ever. She toyed with a ginger biscuit, licking small bits round the edges to make it soft before she trusted it to her small, white, unsteady teeth. I wondered if she was deaf, or dumb, or both.

'There's nothing the matter with Edith, is there, Edith?' Mrs Fox shouted at me, suddenly, above the music. 'She just gets overawed by London, you know. Well, I mean, wouldn't you if you'd been in the Gulliver nine years?'

I nodded. She picked up a slice of supermarket chocolate cake, held it close to her face to approve it, and spoke more quietly.

'And I was wondering why you are wearing so much black, at your age?'

I wore the black cotton dress I had quickly bought that morning, and a black wool beret with a pom-pom on top that Jonathan had bought me in Switzerland for snow-balling. I took it off, shook out my hair, and explained I'd been to a funeral.

She asked who had died. I knew the name would mean nothing to her, but she seemed to anticipate a truthful answer. I told her Richard Storm.

'Oh.' She was disappointed. 'I don't know why, but I thought it might have been one of Henry's friends. They're dying all over the place, these days, I hear. Was this a much younger man, then?'

'Forty two. He died of a heart attack.'

'Any relation?'

'My first husband.'

'You mean the one up there?' She looked towards the picture. 'Oh lord, your first husband. Well, I suppose that meant you had a hand in the service. Did you give him a good march?' I had had no part in the funeral arrangements, I explained. I had even forgotten who had composed the funeral march played at the service. Mrs Fox clucked with disapproval.

'When Henry died, now,' she said, 'I gave him the best funeral you can imagine. People came from miles round to hear it, didn't they, Edith?' Edith moved her head, perhaps remembering. 'I got the Salvation Army to top up the organ, you know, so that when we went outside with the coffin they could come with us. They played Chopin's funeral march, but, of course, we reached the grave long before they'd finished. So we stood for quite five minutes, wasn't it, Edith? – beside the grave, just marking time. At least, that's what I was doing, just like the Guards. Oh, it was lovely, I can tell you.' She put her cup to her lips but put it down again, smiling, without drinking.

'People said they'd never heard a funeral like it. The vicar, he said it was all against regulations. I had a little trouble with him, but in the end he let me have it my way. – Mind you, he did quite well out of it. I sent him a record – what was it called, Edith? Anyhow, massed brass bands playing folk tunes at the Albert Hall.' She picked up her cup again and drank this time with swift, silent sips like a bird.

'Funnily enough, just as the band stopped we had a lo of aircraft overhead. All screaming, those very big planes – I like the noise they make, high up. As a matter of a fact, I had quite a job to hear the vicar. I was following in my prayer book, but he'd finished *dust to dust* before I got there. I remember thinking how Henry would have laughed.'

The record had come to an end and we could hear the rain. It was five o'clock.

'Come along, Edith,' she cried. 'The bus to Victoria. We're going. No dawdling, now. Your feet have had a good rest.' She pulled on a pair of transparent nylon gloves, then took one of them off again to check with a naked hand the Poppy Day poppy in the brim of her velour hat. Edith Smith rose and made for the door, head down, preserving her silence to the end. At the door, she offered me a clenched hand, tightly packed into an old wool glove. But when I tried to take it, she quickly withdrew it, as if she thought it would repel me, but politeness had forced her to make the gesture.

'Come again,' I said to Mrs Fox.

'Well, I don't know your name, but I might.'

'Lyall. Clare Lyall. How about Tuesday?'

'Mrs Lyall, Tuesday.' She gave a little skip after her sister. 'Tuesday tea. Well, Mrs Lyall, I'm not sure, but I think I could fit in tea on Tuesday.'

'Make it about four thirty,' I said.

'Four thirty, Tuesday. I'll be here, then. Come along, Edith, or you'll miss your coach.'

I opened the front door and Edith shuffled past us out into the rain. She was huddled up like someone on a very cold day, reluctantly independent.

'She never likes going back,' said Mrs Fox. 'You can tell.'

*

When they had gone I went back to the sitting-room, meaning to take the tea tray out to the kitchen. But instead I sat in an arm-chair and looked again at the picture of Richard Storm. On a table beside me was a box of chocolates, liqueur-filled. I chose a heart-shaped one. Rum. My favourite.

It was the last box Matilda had sent me before Richard died. She can't have had any idea, then, when she posted them to me, that he was going to die. I wondered how she had felt, arranging to have his body sent home, by request of his parents, to be cremated in Golders Green. She seemed to have organised everything very efficiently. She had even strapped a large wreath of white wax roses to the coffin with Sellotape, so that they shouldn't fall off during the flight. Mr and Mrs Storm could not, with any decency, have started scraping away at the Sellotape when they received the coffin. So they had had to bear a wreath from his mistress stuck to their son's coffin. It had probably caused them as much anguish as Richard's death.

To me, it no longer mattered that he had died. But I did wish they had pushed him overboard, which he would have liked, instead of decorating his coffin to look like

something from a *smörgåsbord*, and treating him to the
absurdity of this afternoon's performance.

At six o'clock, by the clock whose soft tick was loud in
the silence, I went to the kitchen. I grilled a small,
unappetising chop. Ate it with a packet of heated-up
potato crisps. Drank milk straight from a tri-cornered
container. I sat on the kitchen table and ate the food off
my lap, not because it was comfortable, but because now
Jonathan had gone there was no need to go on laying
those self-conscious places with linen table mats and
Provençal china that he had insisted on our using. There
was nothing I could do about changing the kitchen itself,
though. It was a horror of grape-green Formica tops, and
the tendrils of fiddly green plants curled about the shelves
of the dresser. Jonathan called it an 'interpretation' of a
kitchen we had seen in a magazine. In fact, it was an exact
copy. I had always hated it, just as I had always hated his
study, which had a contrived air of shabbiness about it,
which Jonathan thought a suitable background for a
writer.

I washed up my one plate, simply running it under the
hot tap. Then I took a pile of recipe books from a shelf and
began to read them, page after page, like a novel. Steak
Bordelaise, Moroccon Chicken. Sickening thoughts. Veal
in cream with mushrooms. Worse still. We had had that
for our first dinner party. Jonathan's idea, of course. He
said his mother did it very well and it was an ideal dinner
party dish. I had cooked nervously, leaving him to sniff
round the guests' glasses with a bottle of champagne. But
he couldn't resist breaking off his hospitality, for a
moment, to see how things were doing in the kitchen.
Creeping up behind me, he sloshed half a bottle of sherry
over my shoulder into the frying pan of bubbling cream,

bleary with mushrooms. He said if we were going to entertain, we might as well do it properly. When all the guests had gone, he went on about how perfect it had been, and how you could tell how much they had all enjoyed it. Later that night I was sick: all mushrooms, sherry, cream and veal.

*

At a quarter to nine by the green kitchen clock the telephone rang. David Roberts, a friend of Jonathan's.

'Hello, old thing. I just happened to be somewhere in your direction and wondered if I could take a drink off you?' David was in Public Relations. He made it his business always to be in the right direction at the right time. Reluctantly, I said he could come.

'Splendid, splendid. Long time no see, and all that. Besides, I've got an idea. Be with you in half an hour.'

I didn't like David. He was one of those fringe people Jonathan had picked up somewhere. He was on the fringe of the advertising world, the art world, the cinema. Jonathan had trailed in his wake for a couple of years, lured on by David's promises to help him to success.

'You've got talent, old boy,' David used to say. 'Let me deal with it. I'm having lunch with someone who could help you a lot. Why don't you come along and let me slip him one of your plays?' He had shown one of Jonathan's two plays to numerous people for whom, David believed, they would be just the thing. But each time the project failed. Each time David blamed the failure on himself and promised to think of something else. What he never saw was that Jonathan simply was not good enough. His faith in Jonathan was unshakable, and Jonathan responded eagerly enough to this faith, the expense account lunches, and the whole fringe business of trying to make a break.

David arrived punctually at nine fifteen.

'My old thing.' He pulled back the hair from my forehead and kissed me on the nose. 'Sorry I haven't been round before, but you know how it is. Anyway. You look marvellous, don't you?' He went to the drink tray and poured himself a brandy. He was used to doing this in our house. Jonathan never offered a drink to anyone he thought of as a working friend.

David was a heavy man, Scottish, reddish. The backs of his hands and the back of his neck were furry as mohair. Large pores splattered down his nose. I had often tried counting them while he and Jonathan sat for hours making plans for future success. To-night he wore a well-cut, dark-grey suit, but his solid thighs rounded out the knife creases in the trousers even when he was standing, and his thick ankles bulged over his suede shoes.

He lowered himself on to the sofa, squashing flat the cushion Edith Smith had hardly managed to indent.

'Well, well, well. A lot of water's passed, what, Clare?' I remembered he once told Jonathan that the best way to put people at their ease was to ramble on in clichés for a while. This gave the uncomfortable person the chance to associate himself with you, the comforter, he explained. 'Yes,' he went on, swilling his brandy round in his glass, 'it's tragic when things like this happen. Especially to one's friends. It puts everyone in such a confusion. Whose side should one take? Or shouldn't one take sides? Should one just go on seeing both parties normally and never tell one you've seen the other? I don't know.' He looked distressed. I asked him if he had seen Jonathan.

'Well, yes, as a matter of fact I have.' Plainly he was relieved to be able to come to the point so soon. 'I ran into him the other day. He was just off abroad.'

'Oh?'

'He didn't tell me where to. I forgot to ask him, actually. I was in rather a hurry. We didn't have much chance to talk.' He squeezed a finger between his stiff collar and pulpy neck in some pain. 'This damn boil came up last week. It's still pretty tender. Anyway, Jonathan. The thing is, Clare, he looked pretty awful, I can tell you. Not at all his usual self. He's obviously lost weight and he looked pretty unhealthy. Bloody miserable he was, in fact.'

'Did he tell you everything?'

'No, not all of it. But, well, you know how it is. We're old friends. He can trust me. – I heard his side of the story.'

'Naturally,' I said. There was another pause while he sloshed his brandy about again. Then he finished it in one sudden gulp and stood up.

'Now don't be *difficult*,' he said. 'You know I'm only trying to help.' His hands stirred shiftily in his trouser pockets. 'I quite understand you don't want to talk about it, but I don't think you realise just how upset Jonathan is. Can't you think it over, or write to him, or something? I'd hate to have a suicide on my hands.'

I laughed. 'You're being over-dramatic. And anyway you ought to know Jonathan well enough to know that he's much too disorganised ever to commit suicide. – No, I couldn't write to him. We agreed to have no form of communication for six months, and I'm not going to break the agreement.'

David fingered his boil with clumsy care. 'Oh well, that

seems to be that, then. I won't interfere. But you must see I was just trying to help Jonathan.'

'Quite,' I said.

He shrugged his thick shoulders. 'I'd better go,' he said. 'I promised to look in at a party. A client. I'm trying to think up a campaign for his fruit-flavoured custard powders. Why don't you come?'

I don't know why, but I said I would.

Chapter Two

In the taxi David told me his client had made a fortune out of children's rabbit-fur slippers made in the shape of baby rabbits. With some of this money he had bought a huge, ugly house in Putney whose garden sloped down to the Thames.

It was a warm night and the rain had cleared the air of the heaviness of the afternoon. We walked down the front path between shining laurel bushes. The knocker on the high-waisted front door was a brass rabbit's head. Above it, short-sighted pebble glass panes glinted with light from a full moon. David was still having trouble with his boil. He kept running his finger round the inside of his collar and making the kind of peevish complaints that don't inspire sympathy. Dark crescents of sweat, big as slices of melon, stained the sleeves of his coat.

In the house a woman with an excess of teeth rushed at us with an unintelligible welcome. Client's wife. She led us to a large room that had the slightly incongruous look of a much lived in place that has suddenly been stripped of its furniture.

'Here they all are,' she said, 'I'm sure you know every-one.'

I knew no-one. David's eyes shifted expertly through the crowd and he flicked a few confident smiles of recognition. It seemed that most of the chairs had been stacked away, and guests fought with the singlemindedness of people on a holiday train for those that were left. Those

who stood pressed themselves against the walls for others
to pass. Through the roar of voices no individual fragment
of conversation could be heard. – People communicated
with signs and grimaces so that, individually, each one
looked innocent of contributing to the noise.

'Splendid party,' said David, automatically. He took
my elbow and pushed me towards french windows that
opened onto the garden. Our progress was stopped by a
stringy young man smoking a Gauloise with the arrogant
gestures of people who smoke French cigarettes. David
introduced him as Roddy. Roddy put a sinewy arm
round my waist.

'Roddy'll take care of you,' said David, relieved.

'Try the cauliflower dip,' said Roddy.

We joined a group of lean young men all nibbling bits
of raw cauliflower dipped in pink mayonnaise, and flicking
ash from wherever it fell on their bodies as if they were
performing some private ash-flicking ceremony. Somebody fetched me a drink. One of Roddy's friends said
something I couldn't hear and they all laughed. I left
them.

In the garden people flickered round a barbecue.
Sophisticated hands, flaring with jewellery, stuck out in
primitive gestures towards the fire, holding sausages and
chops. A fat woman in a Spanish shawl, clutching a piece
of raw meat, swayed towards the barbecue. When its heat
touched her she crumpled slowly to the ground, dropping
the meat and a black glass which broke up like soot on the
crazy paving. Red wine flowed among the splinters and
reached the bloody piece of steak. Nobody bothered with
the fat woman. I looked round for help. 'Leave her,'
someone said, and suddenly I didn't care.

I went back to the house. I found a room where people

helped themselves to food from a long trestle table. I wasn't hungry. Should I go home? I sat down next to a girl with flat yellow hair. She was eating *paella* with sullen composure. She looked at me, unsmiling. I realised that by sitting next to her – there was no chair on her other side – I might be decreasing her chances of falling in with a passing man. But I had no energy to move.

In the old days, I had always longed for independence at parties. Jonathan, absurdly proud of me in a crowd, stuck by me all evening. He always found me the most comfortable place in the room to sit, and chose for me what he considered the best things to eat. He fetched me constant drinks. – The only time I could be on my own was while he scrabbled his way to the bar on my behalf. When I stood, he said: let's dance. We always danced round the edges of the room. Jonathan didn't like to be bumped. With him, I had no chance at parties. With Richard, there had been no parties. Except for one magnificent Naval Ball in Southampton before we were married. The tickets had cost three guineas each. I wore blue tulle. The whalebone bodice, puckered with more tulle, was moulded into two inhuman points that made no compromise with my breasts. We waltzed to Strauss most of the night, and Richard smiled cigar breath at me.

'Food?' asked yellow hair. 'I'm Rose. Rose Maclaine. *Paella*'s good.' I helped myself, for something to do, and sat down beside her again. 'I'm waiting for this guy David Roberts. He said he'd meet me here. He said he could help me. He knows a lot of influential people, he says. – I'm an actress, you know, in case you were wondering.' American.

'David Roberts is over there,' I said. He was shuffling towards us with an untidiness of bearing familiar to me from the days when he and Jonathan spent long drinking evenings together. His thick lips climbed slipperily about his teeth and his eyes sprawled greedily over Rose Maclaine. They greeted each other with the sort of enthusiasm peculiar to two people who know they can benefit from one another, and fell into a private form of monosyllabic communication until another friend appeared to interrupt. A tall pale man with black curly hair and black glasses.

'Not an affectation,' said the man, 'a misunderstanding.' He pulled off the glasses. One eye was closed, swollen and blue.

'Joshua Heron, Clare Lyall.' David introduced us, dragging his attention reluctantly from Rose Maclaine. 'I expect you've heard of him.' I hadn't. David was drunker than I had imagined. 'If you don't mind being left with a man with a black eye,' he slurred, 'I'm going to take Rosie off for a dance.'

Joshua Heron and I were left together. I went on eating, spanning out the last few grains of rice on the plate. He sat down beside me and lit a cigarette. The rice came to an end. I had to look at him. He put my empty plate on the floor. I could see my reflection in his black glasses, a pinhead in a halo of pin-prick lights.

'Strawberries?' he asked.

'No thanks.' His right thumb was stained a deep nicotine, like the fingers of a heavy smoker, and the skin was charred and flaky. We remained in unawkward silence, like two people on a bus, while he smoked till there was only an inch of cigarette left. Then he crushed the burning end onto his burnt thumb. At once the tobacco split through the thin paper, dead.

'Why did you do that?'

'The first time you burn your thumb,' he said, 'it hurts. It hurts quite a lot and you get a blister. I was fourteen when I did it originally, for a dare, at school. They quite often dared me to do things they wouldn't do themselves. This great bully called Buzzard, I remember, said he'd report me for smuggling cigarettes in if I didn't do it.' He smiled briefly. 'It was pretty lousy of him, considering he was the one who smoked most of the cigarettes I smuggled.'

'Why do you still do it?'

'Because the blister cleared up and I tried again, privately, and it didn't hurt so much. Then I tried again and again until it became almost painless. In the end I put every cigarette out that way and showed the trick quite casually to Buzzard and his friends. For a short time I was quite a hero.'

David and Rose were fumbling back towards us.

'Let's go,' said Joshua quickly. He led me to the room where the music thumped loudly. We danced. Joshua's body was hot and firm and jerked rhymically as an electric toy. Faces jumped about us at different heights as if sent up by a juggler from the floor. The throb of people dimmed and blurred. Music, rhythm, jogging bodies all flared into one sensation.

'My head's cracking.' Joshua was speaking from a long way off. 'Sorry. Must be something to do with this eye. Let's get some air.' In the garden the warm night was cool after the dancing-room. We came upon the heap of a woman I recognised as the one who had fallen by the barbecue. She sat slumped at the top of a flight of steps, a little apart from everyone else.

'It's Sally,' said Joshua. 'It usually happens later. We'd better see if she wants any help.' We climbed the steps. He bent over her, gently shook her shoulders, and urged

25

her to get up. Her head was in her hands, her hands were supported by her outspread knees. Joshua sat beside her on the step and signalled to me to sit the other side. Together we heaved at her shoulders and slowly she lifted her head. She appeared not to notice either of us, but stared ahead. Her eyes were clear green in a face that was red and swollen as that of a newly drowned woman washed up on a shore.

'It's all over,' she muttered. 'It's all over.' She spoke with deliberate precision. 'Give me a moment to recover. Stay with me. It must not look as if I'm alone.' Her head slumped back into her hands.

'We'll stay,' said Joshua. Sally had trapped one of my hands in hers, and one of Joshua's, so that our fingers met squashed beneath her chin.

'It won't take long.' Joshua turned his black glasses to me. 'She gets like this, but she comes round quickly.' Her neck was exposed between us, dark with stiff private hairs that needed re-shaving. Beyond us, on the river, two swans dipped and recovered their heads from the flat black surface of the water without breaking it.

'What did you do to-day?' said Joshua.

'Went to my first husband's funeral.'

'Oh?' From the opposite bank of the river a mist crept down towards a couple of still, fat boats. I had pins and needles in my fingers. 'She's asleep.' He moved his hand slightly. I could feel the flaky skin of his thumb. 'Cremation?'

'No.'

'Wailing nuns?' He seemed to be smiling.

'He wasn't Catholic.' One of Sally's open sandals slipped off a babyish foot and fell down the steps.

'Have you ever been to a funeral on the Continent?'

'No.'

'They're quite impressive. The nearest foreigners get to any sort of controlled pageantry. The fiestas and parades are pretty vulgar, but the funerals are good. Dignified. I had a landlady once in Rome who was the only genuine funeral fan I've ever met. It was nothing to do with morbid curiosity. She just had this talent for hearing about forthcoming funerals, and off she would go, follow the procession the whole way and come back crying.'

Sally gave a great sigh and her whole body shuddered. Joshua suggested we should try to get her back to the house. We heaved and struggled with her. Finally, with a solid assurance for one so drunk, she stood up. We supported her to a chair on the terrace and left her.

Back in the house people were at half mast, sawn down from their original height. The music was slow and sleazy. Three or four couples were dancing almost without moving, swaying like statues loosely soldered to their base. We danced, clutching at each other with the sadness of two people who are very tired.

Then the client's wife, noisy in taffeta and with lipstick on her teeth, switched on the lights. She said, what about another drink? The other couples took no notice and someone switched the light off again. Through the semi-darkness Joshua and I followed her. We sat on gold chairs, the three of us, round a table. It was suddenly cold. A chewed leg of turkey lay in the ashtray and red wine stained the table cloth. Through the windows the night sky was thinning out, leaving a white mist below. A waiter with a busy face uncorked a bottle of champagne. We drank.

'Here's to,' said the client's wife.

It was funny, that Sellotape on the coffin.

It was funny, David thinking Jonathan would commit suicide.

By now Jonathan would have bought a new typewriter. He might even have found a suitable Roman attic. How funny. Everything was funny. I began to laugh.

'Joke?' asked Joshua, but I didn't answer.

We must have sat there a long time. I ate salted nuts from a cut-glass bowl. I wiped my fingers on the table-cloth when the client's wife wasn't looking. She said Putney was a good neighbourhood to live in. You got the people and the river, she said.

It was daylight when we left. The windscreen of Joshua's car was misted up. I played noughts and crosses on it while he unlocked the door. The engine made a dreadful noise in the quiet early morning. We couldn't speak. Joshua dropped me at the door.

'Your hair's a better colour in daylight,' he said.

In the kitchen the sun was pale on the green Formica surfaces, the fiddly plants and the Provençal china. I started to make breakfast.

Chapter Three

Later that morning I began to look for Joshua. I looked for him in the telephone book and in an old diary of David's that he had left behind a year ago. I looked for him for three days. I bought bundles of newspapers and magazines and scanned them all, in case he was a writer. I read bill-boards outside every theatre, in case he was an actor. I looked for him in the summer crowds at the Serpentine and the Albert Memorial: I wandered by rows of meters looking for his car. But I did not find him.

On the fourth day I went to two cinemas, abandoning the search. When I left the second film, it was evening. A stifling heat rose from the crowded screeching streets: I was stiff from sitting, but full of energy. I walked through Green Park, a bank of deadened noise beside the gush and roar of Piccadilly, and through Hyde Park, trembling with old, stale heat and dust. My eyes were sore from straining to look at every man I passed. As I turned the corner to my own street, still full of energy, I began to run – in case the telephone was ringing, in case there was a letter.

There was a postcard. It lay picture up on the front door-mat – the Changing of the Guard in colour. I snatched it up and ran to the green light of the kitchen to read it. The writing was thin, unfamiliar, and the message sloped sharply upwards.

I came to tea but you were not there, it said. *I will come again. Yours sincerely, Ethel Fox. (Mrs Henry Fox.)*

The telephone began to ring. I let it ring two, three, four times while slowly I walked to the sitting-room.

'Hello?'

'Clare? It's David. I just thought I'd call you up. I spent the weekend in Rome – with, you can guess who.'

'No?'

'Rose Maclaine.'

'Oh.'

'Guess who I ran into in Harry's Bar?'

'I can't.'

'Jonathan.'

'Oh.'

'He's got himself set up very nicely in Rome. He took me to his flat near the Piazza di Spagna. It's got a marvellous view. And he's got a huge new electric type-writer.'

'Good.'

'He asked after you and I said you were all right. You are, aren't you?' He paused. 'He was looking much better, actually. He's put on some of the weight he lost.' I said I was glad. 'I introduced him to Rose. Do you know what he said to her? He said: "If I wasn't married, you'd be a marvellous girl." How's that for loyalty?' It was easiest to agree with him, so I laughed.

When he had finished talking I picked up Mrs Fox's postcard again and looked for an address. But there was none, so I stuck it up on the desk, Guards facing me. *Christopher Robin went down to the Palace.* . . . I made myself a scotch and soda and went to the kitchen for ice. I ran the tray under hot water and flung three cubes into the glass. Last Christmas Jonathan had bought me a plastic pineapple ice-bowl. He knew I wouldn't want it, but it pleased him. 'All we need now,' I had said, sitting at the foot of his parents' Christmas tree, 'is a pair of ice tongs.'

'I'll get you some for our anniversary, darling,' he had said, seriously, and he and his mother had talked about hygiene while it snowed outside.

I threw the tray of ice into the sink, where it clattered and slid about.

'Don't be so *violent*, Clare,' Jonathan used to say.

I carried my drink up the steep, narrow staircase, carpeted with thick, expensive Wilton. I wandered round our bedroom and counted the chintz roses along the pelmet. Seventeen. I knew them by heart. I ran my finger along the fireplace, in and out of the pottery mugs Jonathan had bought in Greece. Dustless. I looked at myself in the old freckled mirror we had bought in an antique shop. Hooded my eyelids, ruffled my hair. I sang a verse of 'Where have all the flowers gone?'. I ran from the bedroom, an invisible wind machine fluttering at the edges of my invisible chiffon skirts. . . . *Long time passing*. The room we had never furnished had two pink walls and two white ones. Shapes of furniture and packing boxes were covered with dustsheets. There was a smell of cheap *pot pourri*. This was to have been the nursery. When I had suggested to Jonathan that it would be nice to have a baby, he had gone out and bought tins of pink paint, and every morning, instead of writing, he painted the walls. He would not believe that I had not conceived, only made the suggestion. When at last he grasped the situation, and no conception took place, he gave up his painting, leaving it half-finished. Instead he bought a huge pink bear – it took a whole morning to choose in Hamleys. 'Just to encourage the idea,' he had said, very pleased with himself. I had thrown it at him in a fury, so he had taken it up to the half-painted room, apologising for his tactlessness. The

31

bear sat now in the undulating countryside of the gingham dustsheets spread over the hillocks of furniture. It had a black wool grin and a red felt tongue and pink velvet paws. I picked it up, clutched it to me, and swept round the room in a wild dance. Round and round the island of covered furniture, singing and swirling, faster and faster.... Then, tripping over a concealed lump, I crashed to the ground and lay panting on the pink carpet. The bear lay within inches from me, still grinning. I thrust it under a dustsheet and got up.

The front-door bell rang, short, sharp, impatient jabs. I ran downstairs and flung it open. The evening sun punctured my eyes. At first, I didn't recognise the tall figure.

'What have you been doing? You've got dust or something all over your face.'

I stepped back and Joshua walked in, passed me, and made for the kitchen. He carried a tall brown paper bag fat with things from a supermarket.

'I've brought enough for three,' he said. 'Cold chicken in jelly, asparagus tips, mock caviar, cottage cheese, ice cream and peppermint lumps. My Calor gas has run out.'

'Enough for three?' I stood beside him while he spread the stuff over the kitchen table.

'Somebody told me you were married.'

'But my husband's away for six months.'

'Then we can be greedy. Where are the glasses?' He rattled through drawers looking for a corkscrew for a bottle of red wine he had also brought. He no longer wore his dark glasses, but huge ordinary ones with heavy black frames that dominated his face. Through them the taut, pale skin of his face sheared away over his cheek bones.

His eyes were wide set, grey and speckled, as if sawdust had been flung into the irises. One eye was still puffy and swollen.

'What happened?' I asked, 'To your eye, I mean.'

'A collision,' he said briefly. 'I've had a bad time since the party, that's why I didn't call you. I had to get a script finished by to-day, and then they cut off my telephone because I had forgotten to pay the bill, and the American producer I am working for kept me up late every night suggesting to me a lot of ideas that I'd already given him every morning.'

'What are you working on?'

'A documentary on rural British life to be shown in Mexico. You may not believe it, but life in British villages still thrives. We've already overrun our schedule by two weeks.'

We ate. Joshua chose his food at random. A peppermint lump, a wing of chicken, cheese, another peppermint lump, caviar on bread. There was no pattern to his eating and in between mouthfuls he snatched at his wine or his cigarette with sharp defensive movements. He concentrated wholly on what he was doing, and seemed to be lost in the kind of trance that comes over people at pompous dinners when the guests beside them are impossible to talk to, and the only thing to do is to become absorbed in the food.

'I don't like this kitchen,' he said, when he had finished. 'Too glossy. How did you get that dirt on your face?'

'I fell over upstairs.' I fingered my face.

'You must have dusty rooms.'

'We do.' I plaited together bits of soft greasy paper off the peppermint lumps.

'What's your husband doing?'

'He's just away, I don't know where. We've separated for six months.'

'Isn't there somewhere more comfortable we could go?'

I led him to the sitting-room. It smelt unused and a little dank.

'There's this.'

'One of you has very chintzy taste.'

'Jonathan.'

'What's he like?' He sat on one of the chintz sofas. I had always disliked them. Now I blushed at owning them, and the warmth of the wine fired through me.

'Once he was furious with me because there wasn't a pile of funny books in the lavatory,' I said. 'He's hopeless. Nothing ever, ever works for him. Something marvellous is always going to happen and it never does. He's crazy about success but he will never be successful because he isn't prepared to work for it. Anyhow, he isn't good enough. What's important to him is to decorate his study to look like what he thinks a writer's study ought to be. Taking authors and editors and agents out to lunch. Changing his typewriter for a newer model. He only actually *writes* for about two hours a week.'

'I get the picture, I think,' Joshua said. 'Why did you marry him?'

'He wasn't like that two years ago. He was always weak. But in the beginning he was kind and undemanding. I really believe I loved him when I married him. But what I don't understand is how one day you can be quite happy loving someone, and the next day things that you never minded before drive you into a screaming frenzy of unreason. I began to loathe things he couldn't help. The shape of the back of his head, the way he wheezed in the morning because of his asthma. When I finally said either

he or I had to go, he crept away without putting up any
sort of fight. He was so reasonable I could have killed him,
suggesting this six-month plan and making financial
arrangements in a quivery voice. Then he packed a couple
of suitcases and gave me an address to send on some shirts
when they came back from the laundry. He kissed me
good-bye and he was crying – can you imagine?' Joshua
nodded but didn't answer. 'He was very kind,' I repeated,
'and stiflingly thoughtful.'

'I've heard it's often something like that, being married.'
He lifted his hand to my head and tweaked at my hair.
'Those are funny colours you've had put in your hair,' he
said. 'Like old straw and greenish hay.' He ran his finger
down my forehead and down my nose, and stopped it
between my lips.

'Shall I bite you?' I asked, without opening my mouth.

'No. Come here and kiss me. I like doing things very
slowly.' He pulled me towards him with a sharp tug and
I felt the fat chintz cushions crackle and flatten beneath
me. Then the front-door bell rang.

Joshua snapped off kissing me and went to answer it. I
could hear him talking to someone but couldn't make out
who it was. He came back to say it was an old woman
who said she was a friend of mine. At that moment Mrs
Fox pushed her way impatiently past him.

'Mrs Lyall,' she cried, 'you know what happened to
me? I knew somehow I'd find you here. I was on my way
back from Leicester Square in the bus – I'd been to see
the new Cliff Richard film, it's lovely – when suddenly I
thought: why don't I buy some food and go to Mrs Lyall
and we'll have a bit of a party? So I jumped off at Hyde
Park Corner and bought a couple of sausage rolls at that
all-night stall ' – she patted a crumpled paper bag – 'and

I had some Kit Kat over from the cinema and, anyway, I thought we could heat up some cocoa . . .' She hesitated, looking at Joshua. 'Or whatever you drink,' she added.

She was wearing the same black coat and hat as before, but this time the Alexandra Rose Day rose replaced the poppy in the crown. She scratched at it with her free hand and waited for my answer. I introduced her to Joshua.

'I'm not an aunt or anything,' she said, screwing up her kid-gloved hand into a tight knot and offering it to him, 'so you needn't worry about that. I met Mrs Lyall on a bench. Now, the problem is, I only have two rolls. What is the best idea for dividing them into three?' She glared nicely up at Joshua.

'Why don't you eat them both yourself?' he suggested quickly. 'We had dinner not so long ago, but we could join you in a drink.'

Mrs Fox approved the idea. We fussed round her arranging a plate, a glass and a place on the sofa. I beat up the cushions which had the squashed look of a finished love scene, but Mrs Fox did not seem to notice. I apologised for having no cocoa in the house. She replied with relief that she would make do with a pink gin. We persuaded her to take off her coat, but her hat had a settled look about it which she evidently had no intention of disturbing. The dress beneath her coat was black crêpe and shapeless, but pinned well down her left bosom was a copper brooch of abstract design. She noticed my looking at it.

'Like it?' she asked. 'I only bought it yesterday. Before, I had so many of these cameo brooches. Henry used to give them to me, one every birthday. Well, I didn't like to tell him, then, but I don't like cameo brooches. They're ageing. Besides, they're gloomy. All those yellow ivory heads. – Anyway, as he's been dead many years now, I thought a decent amount of time had gone by and I could sell them. So I took them to a jeweller who gave me five pounds for the lot. Five pounds for thirteen cameo brooches! So then I went to one of those nice modern shops that has music coming through a grill in the wall, and tables covered with sackcloth instead of counters, and bread baskets and lumps of stone lying about – you know the sort of place I mean. And I found this. The girl there, she was wearing one very like it, and she said to me: "It suits you very well." She said these brooches suit all types. – So I've sent two pounds to Edith and the rest I'll spend on cinemas.'

She bit into a roll and the flaky pastry chipped on to her chin. Joshua crushed the end of his cigarette into his thumb and threw it into the fireplace. Mrs Fox watched him without surprise.

'Henry had his mannerisms, too,' she said. 'He used to make murmury noises in his throat just before he spoke. And if no-one was listening, why, he'd go on rumbling away until they paid attention.' She smiled at the memory and nodded towards the gramophone. 'Couldn't we turn it up?'

Joshua at once increased the volume and the familiar look of content began to unfold over Mrs Fox's face. It became difficult for her to concentrate on talking to us. So we all sat back and listened to the music. When it came to an end she gave a little jump, as if coming back to the present, and forced her attention upon us.

'What I really came here for,' she said, 'was to tell you about Edith.' She paused for a long time, hating to go on. Joshua asked what the matter was.

'She's ill. It's her heart.' She scratched the Alexandra Rose. 'I had a letter from the matron of the Gulliver yesterday morning, the old *bitch*!' She took a crumpled piece of writing-paper from her bag and read: ' "*Dear Miss Fox*" – trust her to get it wrong – "*the doctor advises us to let you know that your sister's heart condition gives rise to anxiety and she must stay in bed. As we do not undertake to look after clients in a serious condition, I write to let you know that we shall have to send her to hospital as soon as there is an available bed. In the meantime I assure you we are doing everything in our power to make her comfortable*" – huh, I know what their power is – "*and I will let you know of any further developments. P.S.*" ' – Mrs Fox spat the letters – ' "*your sister does not complain and seems reasonably happy*".'

'Of course Edith doesn't complain,' she expostulated, 'Edith never speaks to any of them down there.' Now that she had finished reading the letter she sank back into the sofa deflated. 'What shall I do? Edith would die if they put her in a hospital. – That's one thing she's never been able to stand, the smell of disinfectant.'

'Why don't you go down and see the matron and see just how bad your sister is?' said Joshua.

An almost imperceptible reluctance crept over Mrs Fox. 'It's so still there,' she said with distaste. 'They all look at you, those old things, over your knitting. They all look at you all the time and you feel you can't shake their eyes off. – But I will go,' she added, 'if I don't hear in the next few days that she's better. She'll probably recover. She's had these attacks before.' Joshua said that in the circumstances she would probably recover again, before they sent her to hospital. His optimistic view cheered Mrs Fox considerably. She rose to leave, and attacked the government with something of her old vehemence.

'They ought to do something about Old People's Homes,' she cried, 'they're a disgrace to the country.

There ought at least to be some official standard of hygiene, stricter inspections – I don't know. But these so-called private homes are a farce. You must come down to the Gulliver and see for yourselves one day.' She skipped to the door and turned to Joshua with her most winning smile. 'That big noisy-looking car outside,' she said, 'is it yours? Because I'd very much like to go home in it.'

'I'll give you a lift, then,' smiled Joshua, helping her on with her coat. They pranced out together and Mrs Fox smartly lowered herself into the seat making no reference to her agility. Joshua revved up the engine with a roar, and before they moved away I saw that Mrs Fox was swaying to and fro, clapping her hands and laughing with excitement.

Chapter Four

I waited till two in the morning for Joshua to come back. But he didn't appear.

At midday Mrs Fox rang me from a call box. She wanted some geranium seeds for her window box, she said. Could I bring her a packet that afternoon, and stay to tea?

On the bus on the way there I sat behind a man whose head was shaped almost identically to Jonathan's. The same long sandy hair grew in clumps down his neck. Jonathan always wet his hair in the bath, it was so long. He was irritatingly slow in the bath. He would lie back, balancing his cigarette on the rack, and watching the ash grow to obscene lengths and then fall into the soapy water. Later, at breakfast in the green kitchen, he would drop marmalade over the newspapers because he swore he could eat without looking. And then he would stand up with a great performance of sighs and say he had to get down to work. He would drum his fingers inside his trouser pockets so that the knobs of his knuckles bubbled under the cloth like boiling water, and he would say he was thinking.

Oh Jonathan, I hated you sometimes. I hated the way you walked bouncingly on the balls of your feet, exuding a maddening enthusiasm. I hated the habit you had of pulling down your sock and scratching your ankle so that the dry skin flaked on to the carpet and people noticed with disgust. The way you always insisted on tongs for the ice.

'Pick the bloody ice up in your fingers,' I'd scream, and, 'Christ,' you'd say, 'does it really matter?' Did it matter?

I got off the bus clumsy with anger. There was a warm, muggy wind. I was too hot in my mackintosh. I walked slowly.

Mrs Fox lived in a tall Victorian house the colour of tarpaulin. The front door was answered by a fat slack woman with skin the same consistency as sweetbreads. When I asked for Mrs Fox she heaved her low-slung breasts together under one arm, then reinforced the support with the other.

'You might tell her from me to turn that bleeding row off,' she said through toothless gums, jerking her head from the cushion of her shoulders so that for a moment she appeared to have a neck. 'On all day, full blast. Top floor on the left.'

I followed her into the hallway and heard at once the music from Mrs Fox's flat. A Japanese mobile hung from a naked bulb in the ceiling, pivoting like something in a ghost tunnel, throwing spikey reflections onto the blotched yellow walls. I climbed the stone stairs, each one worn down in the middle, and read the names on the varnished doors on each floor: Noble, Eustace, Gray, Hall. Finally, Fox.

I rang the bell and Mrs Fox came to the door. She hadn't turned the wireless down so we didn't speak, but mouthed our greetings silently. She led me to a large room. It was furnished with a huge brass bedstead, an arm-chair, a tapestry stool and a round polished table, all large and solid pieces. In the bookshelves Ian Fleming thrillers were stacked neatly against medical reference books, but these volumes were the only evidence of Mrs Fox's past. There was no frantic clustering together of remaining possessions. On the table stood a jam jar filled with a collection of charitable poppies, flags and roses. A newspaper cutting of Cliff Richard shaking hands with the Queen at a first night was propped up against the dim mirror above the fireplace. The photograph had been carefully stuck onto a piece of cardboard. A reproduction Jackson Pollock hanging over the bed was the only picture in the room, but an empty birdcage hung from a piece of flex near the window, a sprig of dead grounsel wedged between two of its bars.

'I bought the bird,' said Mrs Fox, turning down the wireless, 'but it wouldn't sing. So I let it out. But Mrs Morris – she's the landlady you will have seen downstairs – reported me to the R.S.P.C.A. Well, they sent along an inspector to see me, and the funny thing was he turned out to be a very nice man. We got on like anything. He quite saw the point about my letting a useless bird out – he said he would have done the same, off duty. Canaries are for singing, I said to him, and he agreed. – To cut a long story short, we're now great friends and he comes to see me every now and then. In the spring I'm going to spend a weekend with his family at Epsom.'

She laughed to herself and skipped to the window. 'Are you cold?' The warm wind from outside was filtering into the room and hesitantly she pulled the window a little farther shut. 'The thing is, I like plenty of fresh air in one-room flats because you have no idea how they can smell. Especially old people's. I had to go and see a friend of Ethel's last weekend, down in Highgate, and I had to keep my handkerchief to my nose most of the afternoon. I came away feeling quite sick. I don't know what it is about us, old flesh or something. But then most of my generation have this morbid pride in musty old clothes and rotten treasures, pin cushions made in 1900 and all that sort of thing. Pah! Nostalgia is bad enough in itself, but it's even worse when they have to go and surround themselves with dreadful *in memorium* mementoes. No wonder they smell!' Defiantly she sprayed a tin of air freshener round the room. 'That will do for the moment. Now, sit down some-where. I'll plant the seeds then we'll have tea.' She pull-ed a plastic box from under her bed, filled with neat fresh earth and set it on her knee. She dug a hole in the earth with her finger, very gently, and dropped in the first seed.

I sat on the tapestry stool by the unlit gas fire and watched her. The room flickered with grey shadows, like firelight shadows, from the moving treetops outside. The music on the wireless changed from the wail of a Venetian waltz to an old Benny Goodman record. Mrs Fox was looking down at the hole she was filling in, her web-like eyelids trembling slightly in their downcast position. Her feet tapped in time with the music.

'That was a very nice man, that Joshua,' she said. 'I liked meeting him.' Briefly she glanced up at me, then swooped to her earth again. 'We had a good time. He took me for a lovely drive. He revved up the engine in the tunnel at Hyde Park Corner and hooted his horn. You should have heard the echoes. Then he came right up with me, here. I showed him the bathroom and everything, and he seemed to like it all. Oh yes, he had very good manners,' she went on, 'and he was very interesting about his achievements.'

'What achievements?'

'He didn't say they were achievements, of course. But I could tell. He's made several very successful docu-mentary films, you know. He's been all over the world

43

making them,' she said, expansively vague, 'and they've been shown on television in many different countries. — I had to drag it all out of him. He wasn't very forthcoming. But I understand that when he's made enough money he wants to retire to Finland and write historical biographies in the forest. I said I thought that was a funny thing to want to do, and he said sometimes he thought so, too.'

She went to a small stove in the corner of the room and put on a kettle. We ate small pink biscuits iced with white crowns. Later she said:

'There was a marvellous riot outside the Russian Embassy last Sunday. Did you miss it? Pity. But next Saturday there's a good wedding at St. Martins-in-the-Fields, I hear. I shall enjoy that. You can hear the music right out in Trafalgar Square when it gets going. Once the bride has come out, you know, it's easy enough to slip into a seat and listen to the end of the playing. After a wedding, nobody notices one person going into a church when everyone else is coming out.'

'Did you find out any more about Joshua?' I tried to sound disinterested.

'He lives in Notting Hill Gate. He gave me his address — I have it on a piece of paper somewhere.' She scrabbled about in a drawer. 'Here you are. Take it — go on, keep it.' I put the piece of paper into my bag without looking at it. She filled my cup with tea and unconsciously turned up the wireless again. 'I hear you are parted from your husband for a while,' she shouted merrily above the music. 'Well, if you ask me, you should take a lover while the way is clear. I never had one myself, because if Henry had found out he would have insisted on a duelling match. He was very old-fashioned that way. So I went off to my concerts and parades and things instead. And look what its done to me now.' Automatically, she turned the volume up even louder. 'No, it's better to have a lover when you're young than a neurosis when you're old. Because if you do have lovers when you're young, when you're old, all people will say is that you had a lot of men. They'd probably be envious, but anyone can put up with envy. But if you make do with a substitute, then when you're old people will say: "She's mad, poor thing. She's mad. Dotty about chicken breeding," or whatever it is you take to. So it's better to have lovers when you're young, than pity when you're old.'

Her voice trailed away into the music. I could not think what to shout back. But suddenly she turned to me and snapped:

'They sent round one of those social workers here last week. Pah! She suggested I should join an Old People's Club. She couldn't believe that I could entertain myself. She couldn't believe I wasn't lonely. Interfering old thing. What did I eat? What did I read? She had one of those saintly voices that make me sick. She had *compassion* in her piggy little eyes, too. So I sent her packing, and I don't think she will be back for a long time.' She was laughing again, and making more tea.

I stayed till six. When I left she came with me to the door and the music burst on to the dusky staircase. She leant over the banisters as I walked down the stone stairs. 'Notting Hill Gate,' she called over the banisters, then slammed her door.

Outside the hot muggy wind was gathering force. I began to walk very fast, then to run. Buildings, traffic and people fled past my eyes like ribbons. Familiar shops jigged up and down, almost unrecognisable, as if I was seeing

them from the whirl of a roundabout. I wasn't going fast
enough. I shouted 'Taxi', so loud that people turned
round and looked at me. I gave the taximan the address
on the piece of paper and flung myself lengthwise on the
leather-smelling seat. In order as not to look at our progress through the slow streets I read an advertisement for
a night club in Fulham, nailed to the upturned seat in
front of me, over and over again. I wiped the sweat off
my forehead with the back of my hand.

We stopped at a tall block of flats. The taxi driver took
a long, long time to give me the change. I ran through
thick glass doors into a hall silenced with a thick, patterned
carpet. There were pink tinted mirrors on the walls and I
caught a brief sight of myself: red face, hair askew. The
lift swooshed slowly up to floor fourteen. I ran down
another carpet-silent passage to an anonymous brown
door. I rang a shrill bell, waited. I rang again and the
door opened. Joshua stood there, his shirt sleeves rolled
up, a cigarette between his finger and thumb.

'Oh, it's you.' He didn't seem surprised.

'Mrs Fox gave me your address,' I said.

'I would have rung you if you'd waited. I've been in
Essex all day, filming. You'd better come in.' I followed
him into a square white room sparsely furnished with a
couple of low Scandinavian sofas: in contrast, the sofas
themselves were cluttered with scarlet, orange and purple
cushions. Magazines, typescripts and three penknives
littered the floor. 'Why are you wearing a mackintosh?'

'I thought it was going to rain.'

'How funny,' he said, 'I looked out of the window this
morning and I remember quite distinctly thinking: It's
not going to rain to-day.'

'You were right, then.' I took it off. I felt flat, regretful.

'Come and see my view.' We went to the large windows. London spread to meet the low grey sky. The buildings, a multitude of grubby bulbs, sprouted from indeterminate earth.

'It would be better if they were trees. I don't know why they don't build skyscrapers in the middle of forests. Think what it would be like when the wind blew. Do you want some vodka? It's all I have.' He poured me a drink and fetched ice from the kitchen. I was still sweating. I held the cold glass to my cheeks. They still burned. I told him about my afternoon with Mrs Fox.

'She was extraordinary the night I took her home,' he said. 'She made me drive her through the Hyde Park Tunnel three times, hooting. She laughed like a child.'

'Do you think she can find us here? She gave me the piece of paper with your address.'

Joshua laughed. 'She wrote both my address and telephone number down on the fly leaf of her Bible by her bed, so I wouldn't be surprised if she arrived at any moment.' He sat beside me on one of the low leather sofas. 'Pretty,' he said quietly. 'Rather nice, your untidiness. And you shine.'

'Sweat,' I said, dabbing at my forehead again.

'I was planning to take you out to dinner anyway, so it's funny you turned up. But now you're here, could you cook something while I finish some work? There's a tin of Italian tomatoes, frozen scampi and a Camembert in the kitchen. Could you do something with them? I'll go and buy some wine.'

He worked at a low table and I cooked. Later he pushed the papers from the table and we ate there, me kneeling on the floor. When it became too dark to see we stuck candles

47

on saucers and put them on the table. Joshua said the lighting in the room was bad. The still-hot wind flickered through the open window and almost flattened the flames.

'What does your husband look like? I've been trying to agine.'

'Medium.'

'Height? You mean medium height?'

'Yes.'

'A nice, safe height, medium.'

'Sandy hair.'

'A good colour, sandy. Goes with everything.'

'Green eyes, rather bulgy.'

'Green eyes often bulge.'

'He smokes Olivier cigarettes and wears Old Spice after shave.'

'I would have guessed both those things.' We were rather drunk. 'What big eyes you have, Grannie.' He leant his head over the table near mine. 'And what tempestuous hair when you rattle it about like that.'

'What beautiful eyes *you* have, now the bruises have gone.' I wasn't talking very clearly. He pulled me to join him on the sofa.

'Marriages shouldn't come unfastened as easily as yours,' he said.

'I know,' I said.

'I don't think I shall ever marry. I'm too bad at sharing things. Besides, I like keeping whole areas of my life entirely private – just innocent things, meetings and ideas and so on. But I don't like being questioned and asked to share them.'

'That should be possible, unless you're married to someone abnormally possessive. Jonathan always told me everything, every movement of his day. There was nothing I didn't know about him. It was so tiring, and rather dull. And at the same time he wanted to know just as much about me. He interviewed me when I came back from being out for half an hour.' Joshua's hand was running down my thigh, feeling the muscles. I talked faster. 'He hated me to make any arrangements without asking him. He hated me to spend a party talking to one person in a corner. It was so claustrophobic that sometimes I would go and shut myself up with the suitcases in the attic – the only place he never thought of looking for me – and write terrible things about him on scraps of paper, then burn them, just for relief. Just for the pleasure of knowing he could never know what I had written. Privacy to him was totally meaningless. Inessential.'

'When I was about nine,' said Joshua, 'I built myself a house in a tree in a wood near where we lived.' He took his hand from my leg to describe the tree. 'It was the most private place I have ever known. No-one could see it from the ground. In fact no-one knew which tree it was built in. I'd go there most days and just sit, loving the fact that no-one knew where I was. Sometimes I'd take my collection of penknives there and carve weird shapes out of pieces of wood. Once, in the winter, I spent the night there. I wrapped myself up in a lot of rugs and went to sleep almost immediately – it wasn't a bit frightening. Then in the morning I looked out and it had been snowing. I climbed down the tree and spent a long time running round and round, still wrapped in my rugs, so that my footsteps would be too confusing for anyone who tried to track down my tree.'

'The odd thing about privacy is that although it's desirable it isn't quite so valuable unless other people know that you have something private going on.' I said.

'Quite,' said Joshua. 'I mean, no-one knew where my tree was, that was my secret. But the fact that people knew that I had moments going off, somewhere, made the secret even more important. It wouldn't have been the same, had nobody missed me.'

I thought of Jonathan's compulsive keenness to get at the post before me every morning. He would shuffle through the letters and arrange mine neatly on the breakfast table. He was curious about everything but bills.

'I suppose it's very difficult for people who believe, literally, like Jonathan did, that married people are one, to respect the need for privacy.'

'Exactly. Common sense should help, but on the whole it doesn't, with most people. But you don't have any of those sort of worries if you don't marry.'

The candles guttered low into the saucers. Joshua pulled my head down on to his shoulders. He kissed my forehead and eyes and curved his hand over my breast. 'How would you like,' he said, 'to take my car home, pack a suitcase of things, and come back? Pack quite a big suitcase, then you could stay for some time.'

'That would be practical,' I said. Jonathan had first proposed bed to me on a wet night in Berkeley Square while we waited for a taxi. 'Why don't you come back and have some Horlicks?' he had asked. We had drunk it sitting up in bed like married pensioners.

Joshua jumped up, helped me into my mackintosh, and thrust the car keys into my hand, all very quickly.

'Hurry up,' he said, 'it's already past midnight.'

I drove the car badly, never having driven one like it before. In the house the telephone was ringing. I hurried through the dark to the receiver. Maybe Joshua had changed his mind. It was David Robertson.

'Why are you ringing so late?' I asked.

'Just to tell you, darling, that I'm very happy. Rosie here and I are very happy. We wondered if you would like us to come round and have a drink?' His words were thick and slurred.

'I'm just going out.'

'Just going out at midnight? Oh, I see. I see. We'll come another time then. Did I tell you I saw Jonathan in Rome the other day?'

'Yes, you did.'

'Oh, all right then. Bye.' I slammed the receiver down angrily. Jonathan was gone but David was spying for him. I ran upstairs to our bedroom and switched on the lights, the ugly concealed lights over the bed that Jonathan had insisted upon. On the fireplace, rising from the pottery mugs, stood a sickly blue vase, tall and thin, that Jonathan had bought for me in Greece. It was a very ugly blue in this light. When he bought it Jonathan said to the shop-keeper: 'Very phallic, don't you think?', and laughed. The shopkeeper, who only spoke Greek, didn't understand. So Jonathan repeated his joke in very loud English, con-fusing the shopkeeper even more. I walked away in embarrassment. Later he accused me of being rude.

Now, I picked up the vase, wrapped it in a paper handkerchief, and put it in the waste-paper basket.

I packed quickly, choosing clothes and make-up indis-criminately. The case was so full it was difficult to shut. My hands were trembling.

I went and sat at my dressing-table and looked at myself in the ugly light in the mirror. Once, when we were first married, Jonathan crept up behind me when I was brush-ing my hair at this dressing-table and said,

'Darling, you look so pretty. I'll always be faithful to

51

you.' He must have seen some such moment in a film.

'So will I to you,' I remember answering, ignorantly. Richard Storm, on the other hand, warned me from the first week of our honeymoon that he was full of human weakness, and it wouldn't always be like it was then. I had believed myself and both of them.

I left the room, turned out the lights, and double-locked the front door. This time the car was easier and I drove back fast and noisily to Notting Hill Gate.

I let myself into the front door with Joshua's keys. The sitting-room had been cleared of papers and dinner, and all the lights were on. The uncurtained windows shone blackly, reflecting the harshness of the lights. The room had changed from a soft, seductive setting to one that was cold and mass-produced. I opened the white wooden door into the bedroom. Joshua was sitting up in bed, in an old wool dressing-gown, reading *Newsweek*.

'That was quite quick,' he said, barely looking up. 'There's an empty drawer over there for your things and the bathroom is through that door.' I went back to the sitting-room to turn off the lights. Rain streaked silently down the black windows. Then I went to the kitchen and poured myself a glass of vodka from the fridge, taking a long time.

When I returned to the bedroom Joshua still didn't look up. I unpacked, slowly, stuffing everything in a haphazard way into the small drawer. Then I took my cotton nightdress and tooth things into the bathroom, and shut the door.

It was a small, green-tiled bathroom with a cloudy paned window. Two black towels hung on the rail and a chipped cork bathmat was propped up against the bath.

I undressed, folding my things into small bundles and balancing them on a three-legged stool. On the shelf above the basin lay an electric razor, a tortoiseshell comb and a yellow rubber sponge. I opened the mirrored door of the cupboard on the wall: aspirin, pills in a white box, Optrex and a box of Smarties. I shut it again and stared at my own reflection. A moment later I ran the hot tap so that steam floated up to cloud my vision.

It was warm and very safe in the bathroom. I stood on the cork mat and washed my face in cold water, leaving it to run down my neck and shoulders in small tickling streams. Then I squeezed red and white striped toothpaste onto my brush. It spilled over and fell squashily into the bowl of the basin, a pretty, abstract, pattern. I added more toothpaste to the pattern. Then, with the brush, I lifted up peaks of the paste, testing it like beaten egg-white. The edge of the basin was hard against my hipbone, but I didn't move. I decorated the rest of the bowl with toothpaste flowers: they spread out in a fan-shape from the first, central splodge. Each flower was perfectly formed and took a long time to achieve. For six hours I had done everything fast. Now, time didn't matter.

The basin hurt my hipbone; the toothpaste tube was almost flat. A great dazzling heat sprang into my eyes and the petals of the toothpaste flowers blurred, and merged into one large scarlet and white pattern.

'Can't you squeeze the tube from the bottom?' Jonathan asked every morning. Roman-attic Jonathan with toothpaste nicely squeezed.

'What are you doing?' I quickly turned. Joshua was standing at the door, naked. Behind him the bedroom was in darkness. He looked into the basin, and then at the brush and empty tube in my hand.

53

'Why are you crying?'

'I'm not,' I said.

'All right then, you're not.' He stepped towards me, took the things from my hands and laid them on the edge of the basin. Then he picked me up in his arms like a child and carried me towards the darkness he had come from.

Chapter Five

The rain was no longer black and silent as it had been the night before. It scratched and pattered against the window panes and a diffused grey light pressed through the un-lined curtains. Joshua was still asleep, his back to me. On the table his side of the bed a metal, schoolboy alarm clock and a thin gold watch both said ten to eight. Leaning over to see them I woke him.

'What's the matter? It's too early.' He turned to me and ran an unsleepy hand through my hair and down over my body. I curved towards him. The telephone rang. Joshua swore and flung his other arm out of bed to answer it. I could just hear a high, fast voice on the line.

'Oh Christ,' he said, when the voice at last stopped. 'Well, as a matter of fact she's here. Yes, it does make it easier. . . . I tell you what,' – he was pinching my thigh – 'I have to be on location to-day, but Clare could have my car and take you down there. No, I'm sure she wouldn't mind. Well, if you're up and dressed already, why not come round here and she will meet you downstairs in twenty minutes' time?' He put down the receiver. 'Fuck Mrs Fox.'

'What's happened?'

'Her sister's had a heart attack and she wants to go down there straight away.'

'Why couldn't she go by train?'

'She thought it would be quicker by car.'

'So I've got to take her? In twenty minutes?'

'I'm afraid so, you poor love.' He kissed me. 'I may go back to sleep.' He turned over and immediately slept.

I got up and dresssed, tense with the alert, empty feeling that comes after a sleepless night. The toothpaste flowers in the basin were hard and cracked. I washed them away. Through the kitchen window the sky was a hood of unbroken grey. Rain fell regularly down. The buildings far below were hardly visible. I drank black coffee.

Downstairs Mrs Fox was standing outside the glass doors under her umbrella. The rain dripped and spiralled round her. She wore the same coat and hat as usual, but two goose feathers replaced the poppies and flags. When she saw me she ran down the steps to the car, which was parked some way down the road. I hurried after her and unlocked the door. Inside, I turned on the wipers and pulled out the choke. The car smelt of dank, airless leather, and the rain beat noisily against the windscreen and the soft roof.

'I got this telegram very early this morning,' said Mrs Fox, as we pulled out into the street. 'I knew you wouldn't mind taking me in an emergency.'

'Did they say how she was?'

'No. You know how cruel telegrams are. I think she's bad.'

We sloshed and skidded down the early London streets, through the persistent greyness and the warm rain. The windows of the car steamed up and the de-mister didn't work, so our progress was slow.

'Please hurry,' said Mrs Fox, at a red traffic light. A little later her hand reached for the knobs of the radio. I turned it on for her, loud, and a moment or so later the skin of her face unclasped its tight hold over her bones.

I concentrated on driving. The faulty exhaust, the

engine, and the thumping music on the wireless made too much noise for us to speak. We arrived at Herne Bay sometime mid-morning. Reluctantly, Mrs Fox turned down the wireless a little to direct me.

It still rained hard. In the wet, the buildings of the town were the ugly red of sodden chickens. Despondent black streets ran through rows of cheerless stucco houses. Their owners seemed to have given up the battle against ugliness, and painted the window frames and doors in compromising shades of gloomy greys, browns and greens.

'It's nice here earlier in the summer,' Mrs. Fox said. 'Sometimes they used to wheel Edith down to the front. She liked that.'

The Gulliver was a grey-black house of hideous proportions standing in a row of others identical to it in all but the merest detail. It was approached by a red tile path cut between two patches of scurvy lawn. On one was a large wooden notice which announced in elaborate lettering: *The Gulliver Home for the Aged. All Comforts. For terms please apply to the Matron.* Round the word *Comforts* the sign painter had put four primitive daisies, and their gold paint had run down to *Matron*.

Mrs Fox pranced up the wet path, tapping it distastefully with her umbrella, and rang a rusty handbell. It was answered by a small dark-haired maid with unshaven legs.

'I'm Mrs Fox. My sister, Edith Smith. . .'

'Oh yes, one moment.' The girl hurried away and left us standing in the porch. In front of us was a hall papered with a dim, nubbly paper reminiscent of cheap brocade. The only furniture was a large polished hat-stand and a gilt-framed message that said *Love Your Neighbour* in a whirl of maroon peonies.

'Judging by this hall you might think the place was clean,' said Mrs Fox, prodding the multicoloured tile floor with her umbrella, and spattering it with drops of rain. 'That's why they receive visitors here and don't like them to go any farther.'

A door off the hall opened and a thin, hunch-shouldered woman came towards us. She had rimless glasses and a hairy face. She wore a dress of mauve crotcheted wool, and under this small lumps of breasts, knotted straps and suspenders stood out obscenely.

'Miss Fox,' she said, 'good of you to come. It wasn't worth getting her to hospital, she won't live the day.'

'I'm Mrs Fox. – This is Matron.'

'A relation?' The Matron smiled up at me, stretching her thin bloodless lips over a crowd of ill-formed teeth. 'Would you like to come and see Miss Smith too?' I said no, I was not a relation and I would wait in the hall. But Mrs Fox plucked quickly at my arm.

'Do come,' she whispered. 'Edith would like to see you again.'

The Matron led us down a brown linoleum-covered passage which bulged out at the end into a shapeless inner hall or room.

'The lounge,' she said brightly. With a little clipped movement of her skinny hand she gestured towards a huddle of old people in arm-chairs round a gas fire. Seven pairs of faded eyes moved listlessly towards us. 'They're waiting for their dinner. I always say they're just like farm animals, you know. Up at the gate before the farmer gets there with his basket.' She laughed at her joke and clattered up a flight of narrow wooden stairs. On the landing at the top stood a pile of slop pails, wet rags and chipped enamel bowls. There was a smell of disinfectant.

'Didn't you move her room?' asked Mrs Fox, nodding towards a white door. 'You said you would, last time I was here. You knew she never liked the one she's in.'

'My dear Miss Fox,' the Matron replied, 'if I succumbed to even a fraction of the whims of the people in this place I'd be running round on my hands and knees twenty-four hours a day. You ought to be grateful we didn't send her to hospital.'

'My name is *Mrs* Fox.'

The Matron scratched at the white door and opened it curtly. She beckoned us to follow her in.

The blinds of the narrow room were drawn, so that when we first left the beige light of the corridor it was difficult to distinguish anything more than a few weak shapes.

'Hello, Miss Smith. Feeling better?' The Matron's voice vibrated through the semi-darkness. 'How is she, Lillian?' A young girl in nurse's uniform came into focus by the low, narrow bed.

'Not so bad.'

'We might as well let the light in, in spite of the rain, yes?' With the stealthy speed of a cat who knows its way in the dark the Matron moved to the window and snapped up the blind. The square of wet grey light rang through the room with a suddenness that almost shocked. The nurse looked up at us, as we stood cautiously by the bed, and smiled. She had large teeth that squatted on a plump vermilion lower lip. In the dim room the redness of her mouth was dazzling.

'Edith . . .' Mrs Fox put out a gloved hand and poked at the wan lumps under the blanket. Her fingers trailed up the sharp ridge of a leg, stopped at a peak of knee bone. Then, slowly, she made her eyes climb up over the undulations of the shrunken body till they reached the head, propped up on pillows.

'Edith, I'm here.' Edith gave no flicker of recognition. Her milky eyes hovered and trembled under the half-shut lids. The skin of her burned-out face raged under a mauve flush.

'Perhaps we had better leave them together,' suggested the Matron, cheerfully. She clacked her fingernails against the clutter of gauze-covered enamel bowls on the bedside table.

'Yes, you go,' said Mrs Fox to me. With an effort, she moved nearer to her sister. Edith's hand was lying on the blanket, a small bundle of bones tied up in a rag of spotted skin. Mrs Fox picked up this hand and shook it at me.

'Malnutrition,' she said, and let it fall back on to the blanket. Edith blinked very slowly.

The Matron tugged at my sleeve and we left the room.

'They get such funny ideas,' she whispered, spitting, as we went downstairs. 'Sometimes, the relations turn out to be as daft as the inmates.'

In the lounge, the seven old people were seated at a table now, eating some kind of stew out of soup plates. The table was covered with a squashy checked oil cloth, made soft by a blanket beneath. There was a napkin ring in front of each plate; seven plastic glasses, and plastic salt and pepper pots shaped like mushrooms. The room was very quiet, except for the hiss of the gas fire and the slopping noise of gravy being sucked out of spoons.

'Perhaps you would like to wait here for a while,' said the Matron, 'while Mrs Fox makes up her mind what she's going to do.' She indicated a flowered arm-chair. I thanked her, sat down, and picked up a copy of the *Radio Times* from the floor. She went away.

As soon as she had left, with one accord the old people edged round in their chairs to look at me.

'Is Edith gone?' asked one old woman, finally. She wore an apple green cardigan worn smooth as felt from washing. Her chin rested on her bowl of soup.

'No, her sister is with her.'

'If you ask me, she'll hang on for weeks,' said an old man. 'You might think you've come down here for the day, but you might have to stay weeks, or months.' He chuckled to himself. A streak of brown gravy ran down his pitted chin.

'Did she speak to you?' asked the first old woman.

'No, she didn't say a word.'

'She hasn't addressed anyone with a word, let alone a civil one, ever since she's been here. I would have liked to have met someone who had heard her utter.' The old man clawed at the elbow of the green cardigan, shaking with laughter.

'Don't carry on like that, George. Edith was very fond of her sister.'

'I never said she wasn't,' replied George, crumbling into another laugh. 'Anyhow, how could you tell who she was fond of, if she didn't speak?'

'You just could,' said the old woman, dabbing at her eye with her napkin.

The maid came in with a Pyrex dish of prunes and a sauceboat of custard. An old woman nearest to me looked up sharply. She had a pointed head, like a turnip, and a thin clump of white hair crowned the point – the kind of hair that can be snapped off a vegetable with one small gesture before boiling. She wore mittens on her hands. All the time the maid changed the plates and doled out helpings of prunes and custard this old woman followed her

61

with hatred in her spiky eyes. When at last the maid left the room, she banged on the oil cloth with a clenched fist. The noise was no more than a muffled thud.

'In my day,' she said, 'we would rather have gone out to the kitchens and helped ourselves than be waited upon by foreigners.'

'Shut up, Avis,' said George, at once. Avis crooked her finger and picked up her spoon. Opposite her, another white-haired old woman whose skinny neck was pricked by a hundred ropes of sharp black beads, and who looked permanently indignant, chipped into the fight.

'You with your *folly de grander*,' she said, shaking a custardy spoon towards Avis. Then she gave Avis a huge, toothless grin. She had long gums the whitish colour of condensation in a polythene bag.

'How can I expect you to understand?' asked Avis benignly. 'To begin with, you've never had any education. You've never been waited upon in the style my husband and I were accustomed to. Why, we had the finest china and silver and glass in all of Hastings. And Firebird, the butler, used to clean the silver with his thumb, you know. . . .'

'I said lay off, Avis,' snapped George. 'If your china and that had been that bloody marvellous, why didn't you sell it? Then you could have retired to a Majestic Hotel somewhere, instead of here, and surrounded yourself with other fine-china ladies who would have appreciated you.' He chuckled again and several of the others joined in.

'You're always sniping,' replied Avis, with a little shudder, as if she was cold.

They left the table and moved slowly back to the faded chairs. The three old men pulled tins of tobacco from the sagging pockets of their cardigans, and lit pipes. Three of the women picked up sewing or knitting. Avis pulled a small plastic sponge bag from down the side of her chair, took from it a silver-backed looking-glass, and dabbed at her white clump of hair. I read the *Radio Times*.

Some time later Mrs Fox reappeared, stiffly upright and walking with a conscious quiet. She ignored the curious glances she attracted and came straight over to my chair.

'I wouldn't want you to wait for me here any longer,' she said, in a voice not too low for all the listeners to hear, 'I'll direct you to the Golden Sands. You can make arrangements from there, and have tea. They have the television on nearly all the time,' she added.

She came with me to the front door and I promised to wait for her at the hotel. 'It will only be a few hours,' she said.

The Golden Sands was clumsily built of black and greasy stone. It overlooked a long sweep of grey beach and a lustreless sea. Inside, the walls were the colour of old teeth and a sports programme on the television blared through the soggy atmosphere.

I went to the reception desk and asked to use the telephone. The receptionist, dressed like a stage parlourmaid, directed me to behind a Japanese screen in the hall. When I explained I wanted to get through to London, she did not hold much promise for my call. She was right. The line wheezed and spluttered, and the girl on the exchange could barely hear me. Finally Joshua's number rang, distantly, fifteen times. No reply.

I went to the lounge. As there was no one else there, I turned off the television. I sat in a brown damask chair and lit a cigarette. The receptionist brought me a tray with a

63

plate of rock cakes and a china teapot painted to look like miniature bricks.

'I'm everything here,' she said, banging the tray on to the table. It was ten to four.

Several years ago Richard Storm and I had stayed in a hotel similar to the Golden Sands in Portsmouth. The smell of old furnishings was familiar. We moved there after a bleak, cold honeymoon in a Dorset cottage.

'It will be more convenient,' Richard had said, 'than a flat. The flats aren't very nice in Portsmouth, and you won't have to cook.'

He had taken the best suite, a faded blue room with narrow twin beds and a noisy cupboard, and a pink bath-room where long brown stains ate into the deep bath.

'A lovely view of the harbour,' Richard had said.

Every morning his alarm woke us at seven thirty and he sprang out of bed with a guilty fright that never decreased as the mornings continued. He had a bath, and dressed, as far as his shirt, in the bathroom. Then he returned to put on his naval uniform in front of me. He would ruffle my hair and say he was just off for a bite of breakfast, and take great strides towards the door that made the floor creak. Later he would return, smelling of egg or sausages on alternate days, kiss me on the forehead and wish me a good day. He left *The Guardian* on the bed.

Nine o'clock until ten went by easily enough. I would read the paper and have a long bath; dress slowly and look at the harbour. Then I would go for a walk and buy a paperback, and not let myself look at a clock until I imagined that an hour or so had passed. Sometimes Richard would surprise me by coming back for lunch. He would jaunt into the lounge, where I was waiting for the dining-room to open at twelve thirty, and kiss me on the forehead again. He would take my arm and guide me to the bar. People would look up at us from their drinks and I would feel rather proud. We sat on tall stools and drank a glass of medium dry sherry, and ate a plate of crisps, and the bar took on a small air of excitement which I never could recapture when he wasn't there. He and the barman talked about the sea and winds and knots, and I gazed at Richard's profile through the reflections of bottles and glasses in the mirror behind the bar. Then we would lunch in the stiff, white dining-room – Spaghetti Bolognese served on toast, with sprouts, – and I would listen to a story about a night he spent in a Tahitian brothel. At the end of those sort of stories Richard always laughed guiltily, and said he shouldn't be telling his child wife such things.

In the afternoons I would go to a cinema, or feed the seagulls or have my hair done. Three evenings a week we would drive the yellow Ford Anglia to some local country pub for dinner. Sometimes, I would find a cottage near Portsmouth for Richard to contemplate. The hotel would make us up a box of fishpaste sandwiches and Penguin biscuits, and we would take a picnic to see it on a Sunday. But Richard was never tempted. The isolation or the unruly garden or the lack of heating depressed him. He preferred our hotel life.

When we came back to the hotel in the evenings, never later than ten thirty, it was always asleep. We would talk softly along the passages, and keep our voices low in our room. One night, after Richard had climbed back into his own bed again, he turned on the bedside light. The clock said midnight.

'I want to talk to you,' he said.

'What about?' I was sleepy, and unused to our routine being disturbed.

He leant on his elbow and did his pyjama jacket up to the neck. His ruffled hair stood straight up on his head, grey and stiff.

'I can never forget you're twenty years younger than me, little one, and there's a whole – gap of experience between us.' I thought of myself as a small rowing boat and him as an ocean liner. The rowing boat bounced hopelessly behind the liner, divided from it by a mile of churning sea. I giggled.

'No, seriously,' he said. 'That's what I think. And the thing is,' he paused, 'the thing is, an old sea dog like me isn't likely to change his ways. There's something I've been meaning to tell you ever since we were married. – I'm very ashamed of myself, but I must get it off my chest for once and for all.' He undid his top pyjama button and did it up again. 'Just before I came back from Barcelona to marry you, I was unfaithful to you. I had promised myself never to see Matilda again – but I did.'

I lay back on my pillow and he craned higher up on his elbow to see my face.

'Oh,' I said, 'you mean the girl whose photograph is in your wallet?'

'Now, don't cry and get upset, darling,' he said, extending a huge hand, with fingers outspread, towards me. 'You must understand. I had to tell you.'

I asked about Matilda, and with relief he turned out the light.

'You don't mind, do you?' he asked, and told me about her. She was thirty and divorced. Her skin was permanently suntanned and she smelt of tubor roses. She had black hair and kind eyes and three tom cats, and they had met in a night-club. She had a head like a rock, she cooked like a dream, and she wore tight silk trousers. We talked about her most of the night.

Every day for a week, after that night, Richard returned to lunch with me. We never mentioned Matilda. Instead, we made plans for some future day when we would have a house on the Solent, and three or four children. On the Sunday, Richard complained to the head waiter about the overcooked roast beef. He was not naturally a complainer, and seemed nervous.

On the eighth day he bought me twelve red roses wrapped in cellophane paper, and a box of liqueur chocolates. That evening I drove him down to the ship and waved good-bye. Duty forced him to return to Barcelona.

*

At five to eight Mrs Fox walked quietly into the room. In the subdued light, the dust of rain on her black coat made it glow like moleskin. Her hands were clenched at her side, gloveless.

'Edith is dead,' she said. 'She died fourteen minutes ago.'

I stood up and she sat down.

'Shall I get you some – tea, or brandy or anything?'

'No, no. I'll think about that later.' She stared at the blank television set. I asked if I could help in any way.

'No. You must go back to London. Joshua will be waiting for you. You have already done enough. I must stay here for a few days and arrange things.' She spoke very quietly, with pauses in between each sentence. At a sign from her I turned on the television and we watched a commercial for Quick Brew tea. 'I was thinking,' she went on, 'there might be a band down here, somewhere, who would care to play. . . . What do you think?'

'There might be,' I said, and she smiled. She stood up, came across to me and offered a clenched hand.

'Now please go,' she said, 'and no arguing. I will be all right.' She led me to the door, her hand taut but unquivering. As I left I heard her asking the receptionist for a room from which she could hear the sea.

*

Through the dark the lights crash on to the windscreen. Rosettes of blinding lights that split, multiply, divide and bloom again. The rain splinters the lights into a million petals that stay whole for a moment, then join into mean little channels and sneak down the glass. On another night like this Jonathan, driving in his fur-lined gloves, once said:

'Darling, I must get one of those cloth covers for the steering wheel. . . .' Why should I remember that?

The noise of the engine, the wet black margin of night round the brilliant windscreen. Among the fractured headlights swim the dying Edith's eyes, not quite burnt out. Was she frightened, or was she too tired to be frightened? Did the girl with the vermilion lips close the lids over her eyes when she died? Or was that the Matron's prerogative?

I turn on the wireless. Bud Flanagan is crooning 'Underneath the Arches', and I smile to myself because if I did not smile I would almost cry. But at the end of this journey Joshua would be there with aspirin for the pain in my head, and a drink with ice in it which he would get quickly with no fuss, like a good actor does on the stage.

I could have a bath and talk to him about his day, while he sat on the edge. Then he could take over the driving of the noisy car and we would go to a warm dark restaurant where candles and steaks and wine would crowd out Herne Bay and the ultra-black night. I accelerate. Doubly fast the lights crash on to the windscreen.

*

But Joshua was not in the flat. It was dark. The curtains were undrawn and the bed unmade. I threw myself on to the cold, rumpled bedclothes and shut my eyes. I had no energy to get up again.

It can only have been a few moments later, but it felt like several hours, that he came back. I could hear him in the next room, snapping on lights and flicking shut curtains. I didn't call and he came in.

'Are you asleep?'

'No.' I sat up. He put on the light.

'You look exhausted. Was it awful?'

'It was long.'

'I've had a terrible day, too.' He sat beside me on the bed and took off his glasses. 'In the cutting-room. Most of the good bits are on the floor.'

'I'm very hungry,' I said. 'Is there any food?'

'Not a thing. There's a coffee bar place where we could get an omelette downstairs. We'd better hurry, before it shuts.'

We drank neat vodka. Warmth began to ease out the empty tiredness and the room became as fluid as an underwater scene. In the lift Joshua held my hand. In return I leant against him, half for support.

The coffee bar was almost empty. We sat in a corner by the window at a Formica-topped table and I focused on the island of salt, pepper and tomato sauce in its middle. A waitress with a squint approached us.

'There's only omelettes left, you can have,' she said, with some triumph.

'We only want omelettes – they are the only thing in the world we want,' said Joshua, 'if you could give us the choice of everything, if you could set a banquet before us, all us would ask for is an omelette. Think of what you could tempt us with: whole sucking pigs turning on a spit – '

'Sucking what?' said the waitress, making a note on her pad.

'Sucking pigs. And wild boar and linnets' tongues, gulls' eggs and *boeuf en croute* and caviar; *fraises de bois* soaked in champagne and *tagliatelle verde*; and crumpets and waffles with maple syrup and steak tartare and *marrons glacés*. . .'

'That'll be omelettes for two, then,' said the waitress, and almost ran away. We laughed weakly and pushed the salt and pepper and tomato sauce away to hold hands again, and the grainy pattern of the Formica blurred like rain.

'Do you invite lots of girls back to your flat – to stay?' I asked.

'Hundreds of thousands,' said Joshua.

'Why have you asked me to stay? How long can I stay for?'

'I don't know. The thing about you – ' He shrugged. 'The thing with you, when you're not there I don't have to think about you very much. When you're there, it's so strong. I mean to-day, working, I didn't think about you at all. Not till I was coming home. Then I remembered, and it was something nice to look forward to.'

'Well, I thought about you,' I said.

'What did you think?'

'It was while I was waiting in the hotel Mrs Fox sent me to while she waited for her sister to die. I just wanted you to be there very much. I tried to telephone you, but you weren't there. It was a very dingy hotel with flowered calendars on the wall – '

'It's absolutely no use telling me,' he said, 'there's never any use in telling someone how you felt about them when they weren't there. Reported feelings don't carry. They become embarrassing when you try to recount them. The emphasis gets all wrong. Maybe I'm just biased – ' he smiled, 'but once I left someone at a station. – Stations are awful for making one feel: I must remember to tell her how I felt when she left. Anyhow, once the train was on its way I wrote her a long letter describing the gloom that came over me as she disappeared out of sight. I was only twenty and I posted it, I remember, at the first stop – Didcot. Of course, this girl completely misunderstood me. She wrote back and said she hadn't realised the extent of my feelings, and she presumed that if I felt like *that* about her, I wanted to marry her. Silly idiot. I didn't feel like that about her in general. I just felt like that about her when the train left. – That's what I mean.'

'There are whole areas about people you should never get to know about,' I said, 'however involved you are with them. Once I went out with a very sophisticated sort of man, something to do with films, who took me to the Caprice all the time and ordered Lobster Newburg for me without asking if I wanted it. He was very steely and rather frightening, and I would have done anything for him. Then one day he asked me, at the Caprice, if I knew of any good launderettes in the Cromwell Road. I said why, and he said because since he'd lost his housekeeper his dirty linen had been piling up and he didn't know what to do about it. The thought of this glossy, important man wandering about the Cromwell Road with his bag of dirty socks, hopelessly looking for a launderette, was completely disillusioning. So disappointing that I never went out with him again. He shouldn't have told me.'

'It's all the same sort of thing,' said Joshua. The waitress brought our omelettes. She put two white, frothy coffees down on the table as well.

'You didn't mention them in the banquet,' she said, her humour recovered, 'but I thought I'd better get them before the machine man goes home.' We laughed with her and ate hurriedly.

It was very late when we got back. We made the bed.

'It seems as if I've been here ten years, not twenty-four hours,' I said.

'You must forget to-day quickly. It can't have been much fun for you.'

'In a way, it's made it much better, getting back.'

When we went to bed, we curved into each other and slept at once.

Chapter Six

Joshua liked treacle and cream on his cereal for breakfast. He would pace round the room in his dressing-gown, holding the bowl, and stop to look out of the windows as he ate. In contrast to all the sweetness of the cereal, the other half of his breakfast was a large tin mug of sugarless black coffee. He would leave this on the low table and drink it when all the steam had gone and it was nearly cold.

It was a morning three or four weeks after Edith Smith's death. I was lying on the floor at breakfast time selecting stories from the papers to read to him. He was wandering round me, as usual, making no comment. It was October now, and the early sky, as if it had absorbed something from the grey shimmer of London below it, was a sombre blue. Joshua stopped at the window and looked down.

'The flower woman,' he exclaimed. 'She hasn't been by for a month.' He ran from the flat, still in his dressing-gown, no pyjamas beneath. I called after him but he didn't reply. I looked out of the window but couldn't see the flower woman he had seen.

He came back ten minutes later carrying a wooden box filled with pots of chrysanthemums. They were pink, gold, and deep wine red.

'Look! I almost bought her out.' He was ridiculously pleased. 'Do you like them? Do you like chrysanthemums? Where shall I put them? – Wait, stay there. Stay on the floor.' He knelt down, put the box on the floor, and began to take the pots of plants from it one by one. With them he made a barrier round me and the papers.

'Child,' I said.

'Don't you like them?'

'Of course I do.'

'Which colour best?'

'Gold.'

'So do I. Look, now you're in a fortress. I can't get you.'

'If I put my head on the floor you couldn't even see me unless you knelt up and peered over. They're so tall.'

'I could crush down the barrier.'

'Don't spoil the flowers – '

'To hell with the flowers – '. He parted several plants with the quick gesture of someone pulling back curtains and they scattered on the floor. They fell on their sides. Thin green stalks snapped, leaves bent, and crumbs of earth trickled from the cheap plastic pots.

'Joshua!' The papers crackled beneath us.

'Darling.' It was the first time he had ever said that. We lay in the middle of the ruined fortress of flowers. The plants that still stood were tall as trees, their petals bright balloons against the white walls of the room.

'Say that again,' I said.

'Darling, darling, darling. There you are.'

'Why haven't you ever said it before?'

'You always ask silly questions.'

'Joshua? – '

'Be quiet.' I was, for a moment.

'Joshua. You know what? I haven't thought about Jonathan, or being married, for about two weeks now. What must that mean?'

'That something has made you think about him now. What?'

'I don't know. I suppose just that we never used to have breakfast like this. He liked everything neatly laid on the dining-room table. Boneless kippers were his favourite food. Typical. He thought acts like boning fish were a waste of his time.'

Joshua pulled himself up on one elbow and took the cup of cold coffee from the low table.

'Did you ever make love after breakfast?'

'Not if he was already dressed. Sometimes he thought about it – I could tell the evening before, and he went about with a funny sort of smile so I knew that he was planning it all elaborately. He would come down to breakfast in his dressing-gown, and his pyjama tops undone so that I could see the St Christopher on his chest. The only thing was, he had shaved, so the uncalculated look was rather spoiled. When he got to about the toast and marmalade he would suggest that we went back to bed to *sleep* for an hour. He could never just say: let's go and make love. And if I hadn't realised about his plan, and had dressed, myself, he wouldn't say a thing – He could never bear to ask me to undress.'

Joshua lay back on the papers again.

'You know something nice?' he said quietly, shutting his eyes 'The film is nearly finished. And I thought when it was quite finished I might take you away somewhere for a few days.' He pulled my head on to his chest. His dressing-gown smelt of damp corn.

'Where would we go? France? No, I hate France. Please not there. Italy would be lovely. I could show you Florence or Rome. I know all those hills near Florence - I know farmhouses where you can just drop in and they fry you plates of bacon – Or we could try Spain, perhaps, or Corfu. Corfu's like Gloucestershire in the summer.'

'None of those places, baby,' he said.

'Where, then?'

'Norfolk.'

'Norfolk?'

'It's marvellous.'

'I don't know it.'

'You will. You'll like it.'

'But the weather?'

'It'll be rather dank, and quite cold in the evenings. I have a small boat up there. We'll take her out to the island and have picnic lunches. You could build a fire, even.' I could see him smiling to himself, his eyes still shut.

'A fire? Me? Won't it be too cold for outdoor cooking? How will we go? In the car?'

'My darling.' He sat up now and dragged me with him. 'You have an ad-type mind. I can see you imagining us in the red car, open, hair streaming in the wind . . . petrol people. The car is going to be repaired.'

I hit him and squealed. He flung me back on to the floor again.

'We're going by train,' he said, and the last of the flowers fell over.

We did go by train, a few days later. At the station Joshua did things quite differently from Jonathan. Jonathan always made a great show of organising the luggage, even if it was only two cases. He told the porter the time of the train two or three times. He told him which cases to put on which part of the luggage rack, then rubbed the coins noisily together before tipping the man with an air of great benevolence. Joshua's way was to carry all four cases himself and to discourage any helpful-looking porter with a scowl.

We found a carriage to ourselves.

'Are you glad we're going to Norfolk?' Joshua seemed distant, irritable.

'I wouldn't mind where we were going.' Witless answer, I thought. But he kissed me. The map on the wall of Southern England and the B.R.'s embroidered on the antimacassars spun about.

It was a clear, hard day. The fields we rattled through were mistless, the trees and hedges turning brown and gold. People on the platforms of small stations stamped their feet and rolled their hands about in their pockets. Joshua read the law reports in *The Times*. Jonathan's enthusiasm for train journeys was too devouring to allow him to read. Not one acre of the country we passed through could escape some boring observation.

'Darling, look at that spire – Norman, I should say.' 'The last time I passed through Cambridge Timothy was telling me about his electronics business . . .' 'Look! There's a '28 Sunbeam Talbot just like the one my father had . . . darling, do you ever listen to me?'

If by chance he was not sitting by the window the steward and the ticket collector would become his prey. As the steward approached the carriage Jonathan would tap a coin on the door and signal to him to stop.

'Let us know in plenty of time when the second lunch is ready, will you?' he would ask.

'That is my job, sir,' the steward would reply – He had been snubbed by many stewards on many trains, but it made no difference – Joshua was quite quiet all the way to Norfolk.

At the station an old taxi, whose seats were worn into deep shabby troughs, waited for us. The driver greeted Joshua with enthusiasm and reminded him of past holidays. The hotel was a rambling, pebble-dash building hidden from the main road by a high wall. A short gravel drive edged with trim grass led up to it. Chrysanthemums the colour of vintage marmalade were clumped in neat borders at each side of the heavy front door. Inside, the hall smelt of wet mackintoshes. The receptionist welcomed Joshua with no less pleasure than the taxi driver.

'I'll get Rita to show you to your room,' she said. She rang a small brass bell shaped like a labrador's head, and a young, plump girl wearing a short black skirt and a bad op-art shirt appeared. She had dark curly hair, slanting brown eyes and dimples even before she smiled.

'Hello, Mr Heron,' she dimpled. 'I heard you were coming so I persuaded them to put you in your usual room. I know you like it best.' She giggled, and glanced at me without interest.

'That was very thoughtful,' Joshua said. We followed Rita along husky passages whose floors, like the taxi seats, were worn into troughs, but shallower. Rita waggled her fat behind and trailed her pudgy fingers provocatively up the oak banister.

'There.' She opened the door and walked ahead of us. 'You'll find it just the same. Nothing about *the room* has changed.' She giggled again.

'Thank you,' said Joshua briefly, and for a moment held her glance.

'If there's anything you want, you know where to find me.' She closed the door behind her slowly.

The room was furnished very simply: two scrubbed pine chairs, a painted chest of drawers, a desk, two single beds which sank in the middle. Their covers were white damask, like unstarched table cloths. The air wasn't positively damp, but the carpets, the beds, even the walls gave the impression that if you touched them they would feel softer than you would expect.

I went to the window. A lawn sloped down to the creek. The tide was out. Small boats lay on their sides in the mud and a couple of seagulls rose and fell across the grey sky as if perched on an invisible wave.

'How many girls have you brought here?' I asked, crossly.

'Will you do something for me?' Joshua came up behind me, his voice patient. 'Will you, while we are here, stop imagining my past? Can't you stop being jealous of my past?'

'I'm not jealous.'

'What difference would it make if I had brought a hundred different girls to this very room? It wouldn't take away from how it will be here for you and me.'

'But that girl, Rita – '

'If you're silly enough to be upset by anything she says, I'm surprised. Come on, don't be silly.' He took my hand and dragged me from the window, smiling. 'Do you know what I like best about this place? It's the only hotel 1 know where they provide free sealing-wax. Look here.' I laughed, forgetting Rita.

We went to the desk. Two sticks of red sealing-wax and a small, half-gutted candle in a china holder lay on the blotter. Joshua sat on the chair at the desk and lit the candle.

'I used to play a game with sealing-wax when I was a child. I wonder if I can do it now?' He opened a pad of soggy writing-paper, cheaply stamped with the name of the hotel, and held a stick of wax over the flame. It softened, curved, and dripped into a large blob on the paper. A string of white smoke rose up to us, with the crisp mystical smell peculiar to hot sealing-wax. Quickly Joshua picked up a sharp pencil, also provided free, and wrote on the wax *I am Josh* . . . it hardened. Another letter was impossible.

'I used to be able to write my whole name,' he said. 'You try.' I sat on his knee and he made a new pool of wax for me. But I only managed as far as *I am Cl* . . . Then he wrote *We are* . . . in a third blob.

'I can't think what,' he said, watching the wax harden while he thought. I took the pencil from him and on yet another pool of wax wrote *We are us*.

'What silly things people do,' Joshua said. I slipped on to the floor and sat there with my head on his knee. A thin shadow of smoke still hung in the air, and the candle spluttered out. We stayed there, without speaking, till darkness filled the room. Then we had to stumble about, tripping over things, looking for the lights.

After dinner we went into the lounge. It was not conducive to a gay evening. In one corner a middle-aged woman vigorously attacked a piece of tapestry, as if she were mending a sail. In the other corner her husband's thick-set tweed legs and a beam of pipe smoke stuck out at different angles from behind a sporting paper. Joshua suggested we should go down to the quay.

The night was cold, almost frosty. A full moon lit our way down the narrow village street, and then down the cobbled way to the quay. No-one else was about. Joshua wore rubber-soled shoes and walked quite silently. My shoes made an irritating clatter.

Several large fishing boats were drawn up on to the quay: they sheltered round a huge Tarmaced barge. It was turned upside down, and looked like a prefabricated hut. In the water, the collection of small boats which had been cast on their sides in the mud had now regained their dignity. From time to time they twitched a little, when the water moved beneath them, then fell back into stillness.

Suddenly Joshua, who had been holding my arm, let go and ran away. I spun round to see what had happened.

I called him. No answer. I was faced by more empty boats, standing like high empty husks, and a confusion of thick black shadows. I looked up to the sky. For a moment the full moon balanced on a mast, a saucer on a juggler's stick. Then a black cloud straggled across its face, hiding all but the barest outlines of the place. I called again. This time there was a weird, high pitched wail for an answer:

'Here I a – m.' It was impossible to tell where the voice was coming from. I felt my way over to the upturned barge, stumbling through the smaller boats, bumping their sides.

'*Where?*'

'*Here.*' The voice was behind me now, not near the barge after all. I turned. The clouds cleared the moon again. The boats were empty. Then a figure leapt from the bottom of one of them, screaming with laughter, a ragged silhouette against the sky. It flopped back and the laughter stopped. I jumped with fright, knowing at once the stupidity of my fear. I put out a hand, groping for something to hold on to, and hit the hard belly of the barge. It was lumpy and damp. I shivered and tried to laugh.

'Please come out now. You gave me an awful fright. . . . Joshua?' No answer, and new clouds increased their speed towards the moon. Clumsily I ran to the boat he had jumped from. He was not hiding in the bottom. Nothing there but a long thin pool of water shining flatly as old glass.

'I didn't see you get out,' I called, and repeated myself

louder. 'Come on, let's go back. Don't let's play this game
any longer. I'm cold. Please. . . .'

'*Please come out now.*' A high treble voice mocked mine.
Once more it seemed to come from behind the barge. But
the moon was re-blotted out, and the darkness more intense
after the spell of brightness. All sense of direction left me.
I clung to the boat I stood by, shivering with cold.

'You can go on playing your silly game by yourself.
I'm going back . . .' I shouted, and didn't move. Long,
slow moments passed. Then an ice-cold hand touched my
cheek. I screamed. Joshua laughed.

'Don't you like playing hide-and-seek?' he asked, in his
normal voice. I flung myself against him, angry and
relieved.

'No, not in a place like this. Not in a place I don't know.
And anyhow I can't see in the dark, and I hate boats out
of water.'

'Did I really give you a fright? I'm sorry. It was just a
game.' He was incredulous. He kissed my forehead and
eyes.

'You do unsettling things.' For the third or fourth time,
I had lost count, the moon reappeared. I could look up
and see the reassuring hulk of Joshua's shoulders and jaw.
Relief that the game was over was almost as unbearable
as the former silly fear.

'You could have come down here on your own,' I
heard myself saying, 'if you'd wanted to be alone.'
Joshua laughed.

'That wouldn't have been any fun,' he said. 'The fun
was running away from you.' He took my arm. 'Come on,
laugh. I'm back, aren't I?' I laughed. 'I'll bet you anything you like,' he went on, 'I can guess what Jonathan's
game is. – Golf.'

'Right,' I said.

'And what's more, if Jonathan changed from golf to hide-and-seek, he wouldn't be very good at it, because he's not a very sprightly man, is he?'

I laughed again, and in response Joshua speeded up his fantasy.

'He'd have a handicap, wouldn't he? – His running.' He broke away from me and ran a few paces ahead, the fat waddling run of a man clumsy on his feet. 'Like this?'

'Quite like that.' I was laughing hard now. 'Cruel, you are.' He wobbled back to me.

'And I have no doubt,' he said, 'that in the end you will go back to a man who runs like that, won't you?'

'Nonsense,' I said. Pause. 'What makes you think that?'

He didn't answer. We were almost back at the hotel now. It was flushed by orange floodlights: tame, secure, warm.

In our room the coral bar of electric fire was no more than a faint reproach against the cold. Our single beds were intolerably narrow. We pulled all the blankets from one bed on to the other and arranged ourselves to spend an uncomfortable night.

For the time being, we spoke no more of Jonathan.

Chapter Seven

For several days it rained. We went for long walks in the rain, through wide cabbage fields. The huge cold cabbage leaves, some almost plum purple, clacked and clattered against our gum-boots. Joshua said he felt about cabbages like vegetarians feel about meat. He picked a large leaf and shook it, holding it like a bowl. A thousand balls of rain skidded about among the hillocky surface, looking for their holes, like the plastic balls in those children's games in crackers. He could not eat cabbages, Joshua said.

We walked over the sodden marshes smoked up with mist and slimy underfoot. Joshua was mellow, benign, almost expansive. He made me laugh. He held a piece of tarpaulin from a haystack over my head while I wiped his steamed-up glasses on my shirt. We went to the graveyard of a Norman church where he climbed the slippery black trunk of an old yew tree. When he reached the top he battered the coarse branches, so that for a moment part of the tree was shaken out of its lethargy and a few rain drops leaked through its great hood on to the soft, dry earth beneath.

Then at last there was a clear morning. The sky, drained of its cloud and rain, was pale and weak. We went to the beach. There, the high, wind-breaking dunes ran into the sand, and the sand ran into the sea indeterminately as the meeting of water colours. It was still cold, and Joshua began to run. I kept up with him for a while, then he began to outpace me. The wet sand made the going heavy. I slowed down, walked. The distance between us quickly increased. Soon he was no more than a small moving figure.

I turned my back to the sea and walked towards the dunes. Sudden desolation cut through me, like wire through cheese. They were scrawny dunes here, with bald patches of grey white sand between clumps of tough, skinny grass. Twenty years ago, as a melancholy child, a group of children cast me out from their ball game in dunes like these. I had run from them, tears cutting down my cheeks, into the fir woods behind the dunes. I had stamped on the earth and flung myself on the ground, stupidly enraged. Then I found primroses. It began to rain, and I picked them. A long time later I went back to the dunes. The children had gone and the tide was out. I found half a biscuit in my pocket and ate it, and lay on the sand uncaring about time, looking at the flat wet landscape. And then the melancholy rolled away and I was left ashamed.

I looked at the sea now. It didn't work like that any more.

'Joshua!' I shouted out loud. The voice lay flat on the wind, somebody else's voice.

Lumps of drying sand flaked off my boots. I could taste salt on my lips. Where was he? Why clouds again?

It hadn't been like this with Richard Storm. We had been fond of each other. Fond of each other like elderly relations who are accustomed to one another's ways. I was in awe of his age, obedient to him. When he had written to say he was staying in Barcelona with Matilda I had been surprised, but not hurt. He wasn't breaking up a great life between us.

85

It hadn't been like that with Jonathan. His consistent attention, often claustrophobic, was a contrast to desertion. He was always there, a habit, secure, harmless. The November afternoon we married in Caxton Hall was no more elating than many other afternoons we had spent together. We went to the Savoy for dinner and he insisted I ate *à la carte*, although I wanted the *plat du jour*. Within three days of living with him it was obvious he had preconceived ideas about what should be done on what occasions. The *plat du jour* on the honeymoon night was only the start. But marriage with him was just as I imagined it would be, for two years. It was only lately that its emptiness and its irritations, impossible to imagine, had become apparent and then intolerable.

And now Joshua. Why had he run away again? Why did he always tease? I lay down, my face against the chill sand, and the wind scattered my hair over my eyes so that it tickled. Then a hand pulled it away with a tug. I rolled over. Joshua was squatting.

'I've been looking for you everywhere,' he said. 'There weren't any ice creams.' I sat up.

'I didn't want an ice cream. I didn't ask for one. Why did you go? I couldn't keep up.'

'You might have liked one if I'd got one. But they told me the man packed up his stall last week. The season's over.' He lay beside me. 'I must have run a mile.' He smiled, he was pleased. 'I haven't had any exercise like that for ages. I feel marvellous.'

'You're lucky.'

'Why, don't you? What's the matter?'

'You keep running away.'

'Not very seriously. And anyhow I haven't run away for four days – not since the first evening.'

'I don't know what's the matter, really. I'm being inarticulate.'

'You funny, pretty thing. You look nice in the wind.' He brushed sand off my shoulders and pulled me down to join him. 'Nobody ever comes here at this time of year. We'd never be caught.'

'Are you sure?'

'Absolutely sure.'

The tough spiky grass bent all round us and the sand, which was dry in the dunes, swept about us.

*

It was at lunch that Joshua had his idea.

'Why don't we ask Mrs Fox to join us? She must be feeling low.' I had almost forgotten Mrs Fox. Lunch was Irish stew and apple crumble. Rita poured Joshua a glass of lager without asking if he wanted it.

'I don't think she'd want to come. There's not enough noise in Norfolk.'

'I think she'd like it. We could entertain her.'

'We're quite happy entertaining ourselves, aren't we?' I was drinking cider and my head was fuzzy. Rita was polishing spoons very slowly at the sideboard, putting them down silently so that she could hear what we were saying.

'Why don't you want her to come?'

'I'm happy as we are.'

'I thought you weren't.'

'I am.'

'Oh.' I fiddled with the salt, making little mounds with the spoon, then squashing them flat again. 'I'd like to ask her just for a few days,' Joshua said. 'Think how pleased she'd be.' I sighed.

'Mrs Fox's great message is that she never wants to be a nuisance to anybody. You can ask her, but I don't think she'll come. Do what you like, though. But I think it's silly, asking a dotty old woman like her to Norfolk in the autumn. Why don't you ask your mother?' I heard the sarcasm in my voice.

'My mother died when I was seventeen,' said Joshua, 'and I never did anything for her.' Rita started on a pile of knives.

'Oh, I see. You think that making benevolent gestures towards one old woman will compensate for doing nothing for another.'

'I hadn't thought of that. But, no, I don't think that. I'm not a do-gooder, and that's their line of thinking. Charity suddenly comes upon them like religious mania, and they cram in a few years of the gooseberry jam stuff to make up for all the years the idea hadn't occurred to them. – No, the thing is, about Mrs Fox, I like her. She doesn't make me feel guilty if I don't do anything about her. And she doesn't make me feel heroic if I do. You can't say anything more than that about any old person, can you?' I nodded. 'Can I ask her, then?' I said yes.

'Do you mind if I clear?' Rita was bored. We went to the empty, tea-smelling lounge.

'Have you ever thought about the worst thing between the young and the old?' Joshua went on. 'I don't mean all the obvious things, like lack of communication, lack of imagination to understand each other's era. I mean the way they fundamentally drain each other. A daughter looks after her old mother, say, or grandparent. It takes time and energy. The old grandparent feels the uncomfortable disadvantage of having to be looked after. And they are both so confused with duties and responsibilities, that any reserves of spontaneity between them are dried up. Then the motive behind any idea or action between the generations is suspect, for all that the people involved pretend that it isn't. It's so exhausting – it makes so many martyrs. In China, there's a much better system. In the compounds there, it's the natural duty of the young to look after and entertain the old. The responsibility doesn't have a ruinous effect, any more than here the responsibility of a mother towards her child is damaging.'

'But you're being too objective,' I said. 'The young don't look after the old purely out of duty. Love comes into it. A daughter, say, who is fond of her old parents or grandparents, wants to help them. She isn't wholly a martyr.'

'She may not be to begin with. But in cases where love and responsibility are equally balanced, and responsibility means the daily grind of ministering to someone physically, then love is rarely the element that tips the scales.'

'What would you do in that sort of case?' I asked.

'I don't know exactly, as my parents died before the question arose. But I think that I'd have been dutiful to them if I had liked them, and done nothing for them if we'd never got on. I don't believe in loyalty between relations if they don't like each other. To me, that's one of the worst forms of domestic hypocrisy. A great breeding ground for martyrdom. I think the whole pattern of tribal feeling, of families sticking to each other just because they are related, is misconceived. Of course, if they *like* each other as well as being related, that's a different matter. But how many of them do? Do you?'

I thought of my mother, padded in maroon velvet, crocodile shoes and bag to match; her manic Conservatism, her crazy love of pets and sunshine cruises. My father: wispy, blurred, his conscience pulling him from Lords cricket matches back to his fat salaried job in industry; the signed copy of *The Just So Stories* by his bed. I didn't love them, I didn't like them, I didn't see them.

'No,' I said. 'But Jonathan is a perfect example, though, of someone who is embarrassed by his parents because they aren't as pseudo intellectual as he is, and at the same time inextricably bound to them by duty. I don't think he loves them, or has ever thought of loving them. They are just an area in his life that has to be visited. They have to be cared for, like his teeth. – You know how the newspapers always give people good marks for visiting their parents? When they write about a poor undergraduate who has become famous on television, say, they never stop repeating . . . *and he goes to see his parents in Beccles every weekend.* . . . When Jonathan reads one of those sort of reports he's almost overcome with smug pleasure at the thought of doing the same thing himself. And down we go to Somerset again for another look round Major Lyall's pig farm, and Jonathan lectures us all about Nabakov. None of us can argue with him, of course, so he has a clear field. But that's irrelevant.'

'That's the sort of pointless mesh hundreds of thousands of people have got themselves into and endure,' Joshua said.

He went to telegram Mrs Fox.

She arrived the next afternoon. We fetched her from the station in the taxi with the trough seats. She did not appear surprised to have been asked, but she conveyed her pleasure by delighting in everything. A Sailor's Day flag in her usual black hat was her only concession to her new environment.

We had tea in the lounge and she sat opposite us and acted as host, pouring the tea and passing us sandwiches. Any sadness about her sister was concealed. She looked at us with merriment.

'Henry and I nearly went away like you two, once,' she said, 'only in the end we didn't. We just had to imagine it. In those days, our respective families would have been very shocked. But it wasn't the shock that stopped us. It was the lack of opportunity. Never a chance we had! Edith and my mother guarded over me – they would hardly leave me to a private thought, let alone a weekend by the sea with Henry. As for him, he was always so busy, and all his life he put his duty – his patients – before me. So in the end, of course, when we had given up ever hoping for an opportunity, there was only one thing left to do, and we married.'

'How does that work as a reason?' asked Joshua.

'It worked very well in our case. Of course, it would be a very old-fashioned reason to get married to-day, wouldn't it? It seems to me not many modern couples suffer from lack of opportunity!' She looked round curiously to the other people having tea – middle-aged, outdoor people, in wind-smoothed tweeds. People who seemed too big for the small flowered arm-chairs.

'How do they take it – you?' she asked. 'Do they disapprove?'

'I don't think they know, or if they do, I don't think they care,' said Joshua. Then he put his hand on my knee, and kissed me lightly on the cheek. It was one of the few gestures of affection in public he ever made to me.

'Edith, now, she had quite an experience,' went on Mrs Fox. 'In 1919 a solicitor asked her to go to York with him for the weekend. She said no, but she didn't make herself

91

firm enough. – She never was much of a one with words. Anyhow they went, by train, all the way to York. On the way there the solicitor schooled her to tell the hotel receptionist that her name was Edith Freeman, *Mrs* Edith Freeman, and not Miss Edith Smith. Edith promised. But she was a most honest character, and when the time came she couldn't go through with it. She signed Edith Smith in the book and the solicitor gave her such a dig in the ribs that she had a bruise for weeks after. He was mad with rage, and she cried and said she wanted to go home. So he put her on the next train back and he never saw her again. After that, Edith said she'd rather stay a virgin. And she did, till the day she died.' Mrs Fox laughed at her own story.

'I was never very good on the classics,' she continued, 'music was more my line, but there is one author I'm well acquainted with, and that's Jane Austen. Henry loved her. He would read her to me almost every day, every book, time and again. In the end I knew great chunks by heart. And do you know what Jane Austen said about – you?' She waved towards us with a slight movement of her hand, and straightened herself in her chair like a child about to recite a poem. 'She said: "While the imaginations of other people will carry them away to form wrong judgements of our conduct, and to decide on it by slight appearances, one's happiness must in some measure be always at the mercy of chance." '

Three or four of the big tweedy people glanced towards Mrs Fox with some amazement, then returned their eyes to their tea. But Mrs Fox was oblivious to them. 'I have never forgotten that. Why, if Henry had read me that particular bit *before* we were married, I really believe I should have insisted on an opportunity: it would have been justified for me. Oh well . . . perhaps it turned out for the best. But I wouldn't like it,' she bent close to us, 'if your happiness was at the mercy of *these* people.'

'Really, they don't bother us, we don't bother them,' Joshua told her, quietly.

After Mrs Fox's arrival, our lives in Norfolk changed. Joshua was protective towards her, and extended the protection to me. He was more approachable than I had ever known him before. He relaxed. He was mellow, and happy. I felt the same.

Mrs Fox was a perfect third party. Both of us were aware of an increasing affection for her, which we indulged in but never mentioned. It tied us, in a peculiar way, more deeply than living alone together had succeeded in doing.

The days were almost uneventful. We walked, we sailed coldly in Joshua's small boat, we ate large amounts of filling English food. In the evenings Joshua and Mrs Fox played chess or backgammon while I read a book. Mrs Fox wrote innumerable coloured postcards, very slowly, to her friends and her enemies. Really, she explained, it was sitting at the large desk in the lounge that appealed to her: the free writing-paper, and new blotting paper, the pen chained to the ink stand. Every morning she wrote there for an hour or so, newly delighted.

One evening she insisted that we took her to the local pub. She drank three pink gins and ate half a pound of Cashew nuts.

'They're free, aren't they? Henry always said it was immoral to take advantage of free food in pubs and writing-paper in hotels, but I never could agree with him.'

'When I was travelling round the States on very little money,' said Joshua, 'I once lived for a whole week on the

93

free Saltines, ketchup, chutney and water that you get in drug stores. If I hadn't taken advantage, I'd have almost starved.' This cheered Mrs Fox. She began on the Onion Flavoured Crisps.

Joshua and I drank three or four whiskies. Joshua talked to the local squire about his days in the Air Force. We all became warmly drunk, expansive.

'Look here,' said the squire, towards closing time, 'let's not pack in the party now. There's a fair down the road with only a few nights till it closes for the winter. It may not be Battersea, you know, but why don't we see what's cooking down there?'

Mrs Fox gave a high pitched giggle of pleasure and slipped off her high stool.

'A *fair*? Squire, there's nothing in the world I would like more.' The squire, with somewhat unsteady gallantry, took her arm and led us out to his shooting brake.

It was a scraggy little fair, a chipped-paint fair with only half its coloured bulbs working. Music from the merry-go-round screeched into the cold air and bulbs of steam rose from newly made toffee apples. In between the stalls, the earth was crusts of semi-hard mud; the grass worn away. Few people were about. A few half-hearted couples stood with hands in pockets, chins in scarves, looking. Not all the quick-worded cajoling and shouted promises of prizes could persuade them to roll a ball or shoot a tin tiger.

Mrs Fox gave life to the fair. She was what the disheartened stall holders had been waiting for all evening. She pranced from one to another, accurate in her aim, lucky in her guessing, collecting handfuls of small prizes which she stuffed into the squire's pockets. Finally she persuaded him to escort her to the merry-go-round. There she mounted a billowing wooden horse, he took one beside her, the scratchy gramophone blasted pop music, and they galloped away.

Joshua and I went on the swings. They were large, shabby boats with curly manes of wood, bow and stern, their paint pale and cracked. They weren't very high off the ground, but by some trick of light, we balanced midway between the curve of stars in the sky and the lumpy threads of fairground lights. Here, the music was softer. We hummed, and could hear ourselves humming. Joshua, standing looking down at me, worked the swings violently.

'You're beautiful,' he said, suddenly, and I began to laugh. 'No, you're not really. But you look it in this light.' He sat beside me. The swing rocked almost to a standstill by itself, and we laughed and laughed for no particular reason.

We climbed down. The ground was unsteady. I clung to Joshua.

'What's happened to us?'

'We're rather drunk, my beautiful,' he said.

'But I didn't feel like this before we went on the swings.'

'Nor did I. It was the rush of air.' He turned to me, three faces. 'Think,' he said slowly, 'of Jonathan typing in his Roman attic.' The thought shook him with more laughter.

'Sick joke,' I said, and laughed too.

Then suddenly we were quite sober. The lights, the stalls, the red-faced men and the stacks of cheap prizes no longer swung crazily about. They just trembled slightly, like pacified leaves after a storm. But still we clung to one another in a dazed way, unspeaking.

95

Mrs Fox and the squire came round a corner arm in arm.

'That was the best time I have had in years,' said Mrs Fox, her hat askew, her voice familiarly high. 'We rode for twenty five minutes without stopping, and I could have gone on, but the squire couldn't.'

'I had to rescue you from falling off your horse from dizziness,' the squire confessed.

They argued happily. At midnight the squire drove us back to the hotel. He was in no condition to make the sharp turn into the drive.

The flood lighting had been turned off and we made our way up the gravel drive by the murky light of a half moon. Now it was all over, Mrs Fox seemed a little deflated.

'When's your birthday?' she asked Joshua.

'Two weeks to-day,' he told her, after a pause to work it out. 'Why?'

'Then I can give you a party,' she said. 'That will be nice, something to look forward to. It's lucky it's so soon. A lucky chance. I always like to have something to look forward to.' She straightened her back and quickened her pace.

*

We were wakeful. We talked and half-slept for a few hours. At four, Joshua got out of bed.

'I'm going for a walk,' he said. 'Coming?'

Automatically, I asked if I should wake Mrs Fox. She had been everywhere with us since her arrival.

'No, stupid. You're an idiot, sometimes.' He was irritable, unapproachable again, his mood of a few hours ago quite dead.

'Where I'm stupid, I suppose,' I said, 'is ever expecting you to be consistent. You change more quickly than anybody I've ever met. You never remember what you say, or how you've felt. Or if you do, it never makes any difference to you a few hours later.' I was pulling on thick stockings, boots, a duffle coat, by the frail grey light in the window. 'You can't bear the idea of surrendering yourself completely. You get halfway there, and you enjoy it, I know you do. And then you retract.'

'Quite right. But I'm not going to change.'

'It makes you difficult to be with, sometimes.'

He did up my scarf, frowning.

'Shut up,' he said.

We took the narrow wet lane to the marshes. It was very cold. Clumps of mist moved about us. On the horizon, above the thin line of sea, flaming streaks curled back into the sky like edges of burning paper, leaving an opalescent sheen beneath.

Joshua walked very fast so that I had to jog to keep up with him. I complained of a stitch.

'Grumpy,' he said, turning round but not slowing down, 'on such a morning.'

Perversely, he stopped a few yards later and waited for me to catch up with him. He indicated the sky, the view, with a gesture of mock pleasure, as if to kill any intent I may have had to take the beauty seriously. Then his hand swooped to rest on my shoulder.

'They stood there, looking at each other,' he began, in a voice that trembled with mock seriousness, 'there was nothing to say. It was bigger than both of them.'

'Stop sending me up.' I laughed. He smiled.

'You look so hopeful, sometimes,' he said. 'It's enough to put fear into any man's heart.'

97

'Hopeful? Me? What of?'

In answer he cupped my face in his cold hands, observed it seriously, then spoke once more in his spoof voice.

'Mrs Lyall – you know something about yourself? At this time of day, you have the most extraordinarily funny face.'

The mists were rising. He took my arm, and with exaggerated slowness we began to walk back for breakfast.

Chapter Eight

'Clare! Can I come round?' David Roberts, at eight-thirty in the morning. He'd never rung Joshua's flat before.

'Not really. We're hardly up. What's the matter?' Long pause.

'I'm back from Rome.' Joshua was working a small circle of the carpet into fluff with his big toe. 'I got back last night.'

'Was it nice?' I played for time till he was ready to break his news.

'Perfect weather. I saw Jonathan several times. We did a bit of drinking together.' There was something melancholy about his voice.

'How was he?'

'Your coffee's getting cold,' Joshua interrupted.

'Hang on,' I said to David. I put my hand over the speaker.

'Get rid of him,' Joshua said.

'Fine,' said David. 'Very nicely set up indeed.' He paused again. Then: 'Well, it's a pity I can't come round. Perhaps later on.'

'What *is* the matter?'

'Nothing much, really. It's just that I was wrong about Rosie Maclaine.'

'How?'

'Well, Jonathan was right about her, really. He said she was more sexy than trustworthy.'

'What's she done?'

'Stayed in Italy.'

'In Rome?'

'She wouldn't say where. I don't think so.'

Joshua got up off the floor and slammed out of the door. Irritable.

'I'm sorry,' I said to David.

'What was that noise? Don't say *you're* rowing already?'

'Of course not.'

'Well, that's all I had to tell you. I'll call you some time.'

I put down the telephone and looked round the untidy room. There was ash on the carpet, coffee stains on the cushions, books and magazines overlapping everywhere. Alison, who came twice a week, said we didn't give her a chance. We didn't care. Joshua was used to it, didn't notice it. I liked it after the prim tidiness of the mews house.

It was cold, in my dressing-gown. Dank November air. I shut the window and Joshua came back into the room. Dressed, now.

'What does that boring man mean by ringing up at this hour?'

'It's not that early. Rosie Maclaine has apparently left him.'

'What girl in her right mind wouldn't leave him? You needn't have prolonged the conversation.'

'You're hung over,' I said. We'd drunk two bottles of good wine the night before.

'Not at all. I just wanted to get at my own telephone.' He slumped dramatically on to the sofa and dialled a number.

His film was ready for distribution and he was out of work. It didn't suit him. He hated the forced idleness of the days, the fact that there was nowhere he had to be by ten o'clock. A company was negotiating tentatively about a documentary in Mexico, but the negotiations required no more than a couple of telephone calls a week. So Joshua fretted, chain-smoked, read quantities of magazines but never a book. The only time he was at peace was when he carved. In the last week he had made a set of wooden chessmen.

The number he dialled didn't answer. He banged back the receiver, exasperated.

'It's a loathsome day,' he said. Last night, only slightly drunk, we had danced together after dinner, and had fallen back on to the sofa where he sat now, laughing at nothing in particular.

'Why?' He didn't answer. I sat beside him and put my hand on his thigh.

'Leave me alone,' he said. I didn't move my hand so he picked it up, like an impatient housewife who has found some object in the wrong place, and thrust it back at me 'I said leave me alone.'

'What's the matter?' I felt myself irritating him.

'Nothing. Nothing's the matter. I must go.' He got up. I stood too.

'Where?'

'To see people. I must hurry things.' He looked at me distractedly, and rubbed his fist down my nose. 'Sorry. I'm hopeless when I'm not working.' He left quickly, banging the front door behind him. After he'd gone I remembered that to-day was the day of Mrs Fox's party for him. But as I didn't know where he would be, there was no way of reminding him.

*

I was last to arrive at Mrs Fox's party. She met me

eagerly at the door, expecting Joshua to be with me.

'I was just telling the others,' she said, when she saw that he wasn't, 'that I couldn't for the life of me remember how old he was.'

The others sat in a semi-circle of peculiarly assorted chairs. They looked as if they'd been sitting for some time, waiting for something to happen.

I was introduced. First, Cedric Plummer. Huge, kind face, and R.S.P.C.A. badge pinned to his plum satin-type tie. His wife, Nancy, had obviously had her hair in rollers all the morning. It rippled all over her head in curls still dented by kirby-grips.

'We've come up from Epsom,' she said. Beside her sat an enormous old woman, Mrs Plummer senior, who was vigorously enjoying the awesome introductions. She stood up, shook my hand with amazing ferocity, said: 'Don't mind me, dear,' and sat down again with the supreme confidence of an experienced party-goer. In contrast, Mrs Bell, from Highgate, cowered at the introduction, sniffling well back into the arms of her chair.

'Handkerchief,' Mrs Fox whispered to me, smiling. I remembered her story about her sister's friend whose flat smelt. Mrs Bell it was, I suppose.

The mixing of the generations at the party was provided by Philip Cox and his girl-friend Liz. Philip was the talented young baker who had made and elaborately iced the pink and white birthday cake that stood among crêpe paper flowers on the centre table. Mrs Fox was proud of Philip. He, like Mrs Plummer senior, seemed to be at ease with party situations.

'Seeing as I've rustled up that little cake for your old man,' he said, 'I think the least you should do is come and tell me whether I was right to take a risk on marzipan.'

He had beautifully greased hair whipped into waves neat and matching as the iced scallops on the cake. His girl-friend, Liz, watched him continually with harshly made-up eyes, her mouth smiling at everything he said.

The room itself was transformed into a premature Christmas room. Scarlet balloons hung from the empty canary cage, paper chains looped round the brass bed-head, and countless well preserved Alexandra Rose Day roses and Poppy Day poppies were Sellotaped to the walls, the curtains, and the table cloth. There were plates of fatly stuffed bridge-rolls, and intricate things that smacked of Philip's art: pastry tarts spiralling with cream, choco-late eclairs studded with silver balls and a wild choice of brightly iced buns. Two rows of neat cups painted with dragons stood waiting for tea. Orange paper napkins matched the orange of the dragons' tongues. It was ten to five by the clock on the mantelpiece.

I joined the semi-circle, sitting between Mrs Plummer senior and Mrs Bell.

'It's a pity more people don't do birthdays so well any more these days,' said Mrs Plummer, looking hungrily at the cakes. 'When I was young, birthdays were real birth-days.' Opposite us, Philip and Liz twirled little fingers. She nodded towards them. 'These days, birthdays don't mean anything to people like those. There's no respect left for sentiment in the world.'

'But Philip made that magnificent cake,' I said. He heard, and winked at me. Liz scowled.

'Ah, yes, but that's his profession,' said Mrs Plummer. 'Quite different.' Her son leant forward and smiled peacefully.

'Mother has her own views, don't you, Mother?' he said.

'I'll say,' said Nancy.

'Like there was the little matter of Mrs Fox's canary, wasn't there?' went on Cedric.

'*Ced*, don't get on to that again,' said Nancy.

'There was,' said Mrs Plummer senior, 'indeed.'

Cedric pulled himself up to his full sitting height, fingered his R.S.P.C.A. badge, and lowered his mouth.

'I won't go into all that again,' he said. 'Not here. It's not the time or the place. But I would just like to say this. If a canary owner wants to let his, or for that matter her, canary go – then what I say is: he or she should do what he or she feels. Now in the case of our friend Mrs Fox, here, she felt that her particular canary wasn't suited to cage life. She observed that it was pining. So what did she do? Quite simple. Let it out. Gave it its head. Gave it its chance for freedom.'

'Wicked,' snapped his mother. 'Sheer murder, letting it out to be pecked to death by the wild birds of London.'

'Wicked,' agreed Mrs Bell, suddenly lively.

'*Mother*,' snapped Nancy, 'what did you promise us about keeping your views to yourself at a party?'

Mrs Plummer slumped at her daughter-in-law's tone, suddenly deflated.

'And my son an inspector of a wonderful society,' she sighed, almost to herself. 'You wouldn't believe it.' She nudged me to come closer to her. 'The thing is,' she whispered, stretching her hand across her huge stomach, 'once you've had your operation, there's nothing to fall back on.'

Liz, bored, somehow managed to hear the confidence and laughed nastily. She glanced at the clock. Ten past five.

'Your old man's certainly waiting to make his entrance,' she said.

Mrs Fox came in from the kitchen, her hands clenched at her sides as they had been the day Edith died. She caused silence. Everybody looked at her, waiting for some decision.

'I've just put the kettle on,' she said. 'I expect Joshua will be here by the time it's ready. He's probably been held up at work.' She looked to me for confirmation.

'I expect so.' I sounded unconvincing.

'I could do with a cup of tea,' said Liz. 'I'm parched.' She managed to make everything she said sound accusing.

'Yes, that would be very nice,' agreed Mrs Plummer senior, trying again.

'Lovely,' said Mrs Bell.

'Just what we all wanted you to say, Mrs Fox.' Cedric rubbed his hands together, natural master of ceremonies.

Mrs Fox went away. I went with her. In the tiny kitchen her hands trembled on the dragon teapot, milk jug and sugar bowl.

'I expect he's been held up,' she said again.

'I'm very sorry. He's always vague about time.'

'Never mind, we'll start without him and just leave cutting the cake till he comes.'

We went back to the room with the tea. The silence of the waiting people oppressed Mrs Fox immediately. She suggested music, and put on the gramophone. A Strauss waltz blared through the room. Philip and Liz made faces. But protected by the music, there was no need for Mrs Fox to make any announcement. She gestured to everyone to come and help themselves. With the exception of Cedric, who was determined to show his enjoyment in spite of the music, they lumbered to the table uncooperatively. They stacked their small dragon plates high with food and returned to the chairs they had come from. Mrs Fox and I poured the tea.

'Lazy lot,' she whispered. 'You can never rely on people to have a sense of occasion.'

Mrs Fox, eating and drinking nothing herself, looked after her guests with great thought. She stirred Mrs Bell's tea because her hand shook too much to do it herself. She saved the last pink iced bun for Nancy because Nancy was fond of pink. She found a packet of cigarettes for Liz, a chain-smoker, who had none. The music gave them the excuse for no conversation and they ate very quickly. Soon all the food was finished and a second pot of tea made. Then the record came to an end.

'Well,' said Cedric, in charge again now that he could be heard, 'that only leaves the cake.'

Twenty to six on the clock. Still no Joshua. No sound of steps on the stairs.

'So it does.' Mrs Fox feigned some sort of amazement and gave a small laugh. She looked at her audience while they waited for her again to make a decision. 'Perhaps we should have just one more record . . .' Mrs Plummer senior put her huge hands on her huge parted knees.

'Mrs Fox, I don't want to speak out of turn, but speaking for myself I should say that our guest of honour isn't going to honour us after all and we should cut the cake.'

Liz applauded ostentatiously and laughed her nasty laugh. The others joined in the laughter without much reluctance, even Cedric.

'A splendid idea,' he said. 'How about me doing the cutting? Seeing as I'm the man nearest to the age of the absent guest of honour.'

But Mrs Fox was terse with indignation.

'Certainly not,' she snapped. 'If Joshua's not here, the poor man, because of hard work, then Clare shall cut the cake.'

She thrust a long knife at me. The handle was ivory, carved with a lion's head.

'The sort of thing Henry's patients left him in their wills,' she whispered.

I tapped at the icing with the long pointed blade. Suddenly, it was a familiar sensation. With a long pointed blade I had tapped at rock-hard white icing on a cake high with monstrous tiers. Richard Storm's hand, cold and bony, had been on top of mine, guiding. As the knife weighed down, splitting first the icing then slicing faster down through the marzipan and cheap, eggless substance packed with currants, tidy velvet people with feather hats cheered and murmured, and naval men grunted. A new batch of tears slid down my mother's mauve cheeks. I felt my nose prick with sweat, and I felt the burn of indigestion from two glasses of cut-price champagne – my father had always believed in the economics of bulk buying, even for his daughter's wedding.

'Ah!' Richard was saying over and over again, through my veil. 'Ah! What now? What now?' I suggested that we should get away quickly. But he said no, he was enjoying the party: it wasn't every day a man got married.

Hours later, we left, through squawking crowds who threw paper petals in our faces. In the taxi that drove us to the station Richard's hand crept over the seat towards my red tweed thigh.

'We're married now, you know,' I said, trying to smile, 'there's no need to be so cautious.' My voice was high and thin and far away. I covered my hand with his and immediately his fingers wriggled free and scrabbled for protection somewhere up my cuff.

'Slowly does it, my love,' he said, and coughed.

I looked at his translucent face, a map of blue broken veins on the high cheeks, the eyes dim and weak, the handsome pointed nose, the pale lips always lined with an inner rim of saliva – the face of a complete stranger. I heard myself give a great sob. His fingers climbed down my cuff again and clutched my wristwatch instead.

'What's the matter?'

'I don't know. I expect I'm tired. It's been a long day, hasn't it?' He frowned and I sobbed again. 'And you've only kissed me twice since we've been engaged.' That was nothing to do with the matter, but I couldn't think of anything else.

'Is *that* what's worrying you, little one? But we've all the time in the world. We'll make up for it, now. All you have to do is love, honour and obey me in bed, and it'll be quite easy, you'll see.' He laughed at his own joke and gave me a stiff white handkerchief for my eyes.

In the two raining weeks in a Dorset cottage that was our honeymoon, we did make up for my nineteen years of virginity. Every night, among sheets that remained damp even when they were warm, in the dark. Crudely, inadequately. There was no pleasure. It hurt. His wet mouth kissed my temples, never my mouth. He rubbed his long cold feet up and down my legs to warm them. He rocked with horrible noises, holding my ears as if they were handles. Sometimes, I sang to myself till he had finished. Sometimes I tried to remember all the people who had been at the wedding, or all the books I had read that year. When it was over, he snapped the light on again, sat up, and took a thin piece of string from the bedside table.

Then he would tie knots until he felt sleepy – minute reef knots, Granny knots, sheetbend knots. He could tie smaller, neater knots faster than anyone he knew, he said. He had learnt the art as a boy, and never tired of it.

*

I cut easily through the pink and white icing and Mrs Fox took over, chopping the cake into hunks that would keep even her guests going for some time. She put on another record. The eaters couldn't complain because their mouths were so stuffed with cake, which they scooped up with spoons.

*

My second wedding cake was eaten with spoons, too. At one hack with the knife the fragile chocolate icing parted and the innards gushed out.

'It's practically neat rum,' Jonathan had roared. He was rather drunk and pink. He had been drinking since before lunch and now it was six o'clock. Everybody laughed at everything he said. Everybody was very happy. He held my hand all the time, kneading the flesh over my knuckles with hot fingers, and led me round the room introducing me to all his neat friends, most of whom I didn't know. They all said how happy they knew we'd be. It always worked better the second time round, they said. When we got to the door I wrenched myself free of Jonathan and ran to the hotel lavatory. I shut myself in and leant up against the cool pink tiles. A marvellous smell of disinfectant. Then I was very sick – more of my father's even further-cut champagne.

Cold and dizzy, I walked back to the lobby. I looked about, unable to remember the way to the private room of the wedding reception. So I went to the Cocktail Bar and sat on the only free stool at the bar. I asked the barman for a peppermint. My mouth tasted sour.

'Peppermint what, madam?' He was quite friendly.

'Something strong to suck.'

'You're joking, madam. There aren't any slot machines in a place like this. What about a *creme de menthe frappé*?' I agreed. 'Not feeling well? You look a bit shaken.' I agreed again. He pressed crushed ice down into the glass with a spoon. 'There's a hell of a wedding party going on down the corridor,' he chatted on. 'They're drinking dreadful stuff, I hear. Poison anyone.' He looked at me carefully. 'You're not one of them, are you?'

'I'm the bride,' I said.

'No, no,' he said. 'You're joking again, of course. You wouldn't look like that if you were the bride.'

When I got back to the reception, half an hour later, Jonathan was in a state of great agitation. He thought I'd gone already. He thought I'd left him. More jokes were made, and he recovered. That night we ate *sole bonne femme* at a severely white tableclothed table and tried to think of things to say about the Thames looking so glamorous with all the lights. Then with the coffee Jonathan appealed to me never to leave his side again.

'In fact,' he said, digging a hole in a cigar I had hoped he wouldn't smoke, 'I'll see to it you never leave me again. Not so long as we're married.'

And so the claustrophobia set in.

*

Joshua's birthday cake was finished except for the slice that Mrs Fox had wrapped in greaseproof paper, with the one fat candle, for me to take home. Mrs Plummer senior was pulling on her angora beret, and Cedric was beginning to pace about. He was the first one to say good-bye, and thank you, Mrs Fox. It had been a lovely party, he said. The others were swift to copy him, and they all left in a rush.

'They're pleased to be gone, if you ask me,' said Mrs Fox, when she shut the door. 'You can never trust people to make a go of things, can you?'

'I'm sorry,' I said, 'about Joshua. Dreadfully sorry. I can't imagine what happened. The trouble was, I didn't know where he was going, so I couldn't contact him.'

'Now don't think about it, or let him think about it either. People forget to go to parties. What does that matter? What's a party?' She began to clear the things away. I helped her wash up, then we unstuck all the roses and poppies from their places of decoration.

'Shall we listen to a little music? You never did hear my favourite brass band.' 'Land of Hope and Glory' by mass brass bands filled the room. We sat each side of the fire-place. 'What's a party?' she asked, during a quiet phase. 'I ask myself, what's a party?'

When the record came to an end, I left her. At the door she stretched her arms up as if to hug me, then decided against the gesture and let them fall to her side again. I tried to apologise further, but she interrupted quite crossly.

'Off you go, he'll need you to do his supper,' she said. 'And don't get at him. It's of no importance. I mean that.'

Halfway down the stairs I heard the brass bands start up again. Phrases of intense anger filled my mind – anger against Joshua.

It was after eight when I arrived back at the flat, which was empty and dark. As soon as I opened the front door

I could smell strange cigarette smoke. I switched on the light in the sitting-room. It was more than usually untidy. Three ashtrays were filled with the white tips of French cigarettes. All printed with pale brown lipstick marks.

I stood there without moving. Through the blackness of the windows I could see my reflection, quite still. Then I began to walk about the room in swerving patterns. My walk felt very heavy, as if I pushed against a strong current in the sea. I touched things with a floppy hand – the backs of the sofas, the window sill, the picture frames. In the other hand I felt myself crushing the slice of cake in its greaseproof paper.

I stood still again. I began to blink very slowly, to see how heavy I could make my eyelids feel on my eyes. I blinked like a slow mechanical doll. Forty-one times, I counted. Then I went into the bedroom. No-one had been there. No cigarette ends in the ashtrays.

Back in the sitting-room I put the slice of cake on top of a cushion. It balanced for a moment, then fell on to the sofa. So I sat on the sofa and put it on top of the cushion again. The same thing happened. I began to repeat this sliding game faster and faster. Then I heard the key in the lock. Joshua came in.

I stood up. He stopped as soon as he saw me. His eyes bore into mine and held them there, unflinching.

'What?' he said at last.

'Who?' I said. He shrugged.

'It's been a difficult enough day,' he said, carelessly. Then his face turned into three faces, his eyes into two black holes that covered all three faces. I grabbed the still-wrapped slice of cake and threw it at the heads with all my force.

'A bad enough day! So it has. You lousy, stinking,

thoughtless idiot. Mrs Fox goes and does this whole party for you, and you just don't turn up. You just don't turn up!' My shriek filled the room, raw, ugly. 'She goes to all this trouble. All her best friends, a huge cake, everything decorated . . . and then you just don't turn up.' He was shaking me now.

'Stop that noise. Shut up, Clare. Shut up – .'

'I won't shut up!' Children's playground chants in my ears. 'I won't shut up, I won't shut up! It's the worst thing you've ever done to anybody.'

He slapped me hard on the cheek. It stung; it shocked. But I shut up.

'I'm sorry about Mrs Fox's party,' he said quietly. 'I quite forgot about that. I'll do something about it.' I backed away from him. Tears from the pain seemed to have blurred my eyes.

'I'm sure you will. You'll send her flowers – very expensive flowers, I expect, and imagine that will make up for everything.' His face was one face again now, taut and cruel.

'Of course they won't make up for anything, you idiot. I've said I'm sorry.' He took a step towards me, but I backed farther away. 'Do you want me to explain?'

'There's no need. It's quite clear. *Who was she?*' A scream again.

'Please don't shout any more.' His voice was a monotone.

'I said: who was she?' Control, this time.

'She was once my secretary. Annabel Hammond.'

'What was she doing here?'

'We had lunch, then we came back here and talked.'

'Talked?'

'Yes, talked.' The sting in my cheek was dying away,

comfortably, but there was a constriction in my throat. It spread across my chest.

'Have you and Annabel Hammond always just – talked?'

'No, we haven't always just talked.' I undid the bottom button of my mackintosh then did it up again. Two, three times.

'I see,' I said at last.

'So what do you want to do about it?'

'What could I want to do about it – her? There's nothing I can do.'

'I'm sorry if you minded, but there was nothing to mind about.' A feeling of great weakness swelled through my body. I dropped on to the sofa.

'Why did you want to have lunch with her?' I asked. Joshua sighed, trying to be patient.

'I don't know. I really don't. The idea suddenly came to me. I just wanted to see her. She was the person I rang this morning, in front of you, but there was no reply. So I didn't mean it to be a secret. If I had, I would have cleared up the ashtrays, wouldn't I?'

'I suppose so.' The warmth of relief.

'She makes me laugh. I wanted to be laughed out of my mood this morning.'

'Did she succeed?'

'In a way. But how can I keep it up, if you go on like this?'

'I'm sorry.' He sat beside me.

'For heaven's sake. You must meet her some time. You'd like her. She's a great girl.'

'She'd got it all ready for you,' I said. 'So much effort.'

'What do you mean?'

'Mrs Fox.'

'Oh, we're back on Mrs Fox. I'll go and see her later on this evening, I promise.' He took my hand. I marvelled at his picking it up, it was so heavy. 'Does this mean you want to leave me, just because I had lunch with Annabel? – It's difficult to talk to someone with their eyes shut.' I kept them shut.

'Don't you realise?' I asked. 'Don't you realise at all?' Under the lids, complete darkness.

'I'm hungry,' he said. 'Is there anything to eat?' The darkness behind my eyelids broke into flares of scarlet. A plummet swung about the ragged patterns, then fell deeper.

'Mrs Fox sent you a slice of your cake,' I said.

I heard him look about the sofa, then stretch down to the floor to where the package had fallen. I heard him snap off the elastic band, unwrap the greaseproof paper and screw it into a ball. Then I heard him cursing the crumbs and currants that fell into his lap as he ate his piece of birthday cake.

Chapter Nine

Jonathan was dressed up as a pantomime fairy. He wore a wig of long blond ringlets, a white net ballet dress that sparkled, and goose-feather wings. On his feet, pink satin pumps whose laces criss-crossed up his legs to the knees, cutting into the flaky flesh. Over his arm he carried a huge basket covered with a white cloth.

He stood in the centre of a circle of very old men and women, all dressed in pinafores, mortar-boards and tap-shoes. They applauded him and he began to sing:

> *'I've got gooseberry jam for you,*
> *Jam for you,*
> *Jam for you.*
> *I've got gooseberry jam for you*
> *On a cold and frosty morning.'*

He began to skip round the circle, stopping briefly at each old person and handing out a tiny pot of jam, like the pots of jam on trains, from the basket.

> *'Here I come with my gooseberry jam,*
> *My gooseberry jam,*
> *My gooseberry jam.*
> *Here I come with my gooseberry jam*
> *On a cold and frosty morning.'*

They applauded him again, and began to shuffle their feet with quiet metallic taps. Then they joined in the chorus, their voices croaky and out of tune.

'Here he comes with his gooseberry jam,
His gooseberry jam,
His gooseberry jam.
Here he comes with his gooseberry jam
On a cold and frosty morning.'

I woke up with a headache, a sore throat, and aching everywhere. Last time I had had flu, Jonathan had given up any pretence of writing for a whole week, with the excuse of nursing me. He had done it very well. Flowers. Books. A portable television at the end of my bed. He never left the house, except briefly to buy food. He did the cooking himself: steamed soles and baked custards neatly laid on trays with tray cloths. He remembered what medicines I had to take when, and read to me out loud. The fact that he felt he was positively helping someone else seemed to suit him. He became more vivacious than usual. We had no arguments; we were content.

'I feel awful,' I said to Joshua, who stirred.

'Need a doctor?'

'No, but I don't feel much like getting up.'

'You'd better stay in bed, then.' He frowned. 'I won't be able to be with you much. I've a meeting at ten and viewings most of the day. But I'll leave my number wherever I go.'

'Don't worry. I'll be all right.'

When he was dressed Joshua brought me a cup of tea.

'Are you sure you're all right?'

'Absolutely.'

'Take care of yourself. I'll – ring Mrs Fox and tell her to come round and see you.' He kissed me on the forehead. 'Don't want to catch anything. 'Bye.'

When he had gone I went back to sleep, but the fairy Jonathan danced no more.

*

Mrs Fox arrived later in the morning. She pulled up a chair by my bed and kept her hat and coat on.

'It's very Decembery out,' she said. 'Frost in the air. All the shops are filled with Christmas things.' She patted a crumpled paper bag. 'I don't suppose you feel like eating much, but I've bought a few little bits that might tempt you.' She pulled from the bag a honeycomb, six tangerines and a jar of gooseberry jam.

'How funny,' I said. 'Gooseberry jam.'

'It was always Henry's favourite. I used to make it for him myself, in a good gooseberry year. But then he was most particular about what he liked and what he didn't like. He never could stand liver or spinach. My sister Edith was the same about raw onions. She didn't like scarecrows, either. You couldn't get Edith into a field with a scarecrow, not for anything. Not even walking right round the edges.' She patted the Poppy Day poppy in her hat. 'But then there's no accounting for other people's tastes, and there's never any hope of changing them, is there? I never could get Edith or Henry to like music – not in the same way that I do. Edith did try, mind. They both tried, to please me. But they could never get the hang of it. I suppose I got it from my father, myself. He was what you'd call an artist, in his way. He did beautiful little silhouettes of people's profiles – he could have sold them for a fortune, but he never asked for money. He said you couldn't take money for a hobby. He was good on the violin, too. He used to practise in the front room on a Sunday afternoon, all in his best clothes.

He was a very upright figure of a man, my father. Dignified, you'd call him. It was after he died that Edith went so quiet.'

She was quiet herself for a while, fussing kindly about me, shaking the pillows and fetching me a drink.

'I'm no Florence Nightingale,' she smiled. 'I should be, I know, after all those years married to Henry. But to tell the truth, I never got used to illness. It always affected me. I'm ashamed to admit it, but each time a patient of his was near to dying, I was afraid. I'm a religious person, but imagining an after-life is past me. Where are Henry and Edith now, I ask myself? What are they doing? Do they know we're thinking of them? You can drive yourself mad with such questions.'

'So what did you do when Henry died?' She seemed to stiffen, remembering.

'It was all very quick, in the night. A heart attack, it was and' – she snapped her fingers – 'out like a light, before his partner could get to him. Then all his patients began coming in. I don't know what made them come, or how they heard. But they came, and they took over. They arranged everything except for the music. I don't think it was disloyal, really, letting them do it. I mean, he was dead, so what did it matter? Though I often wonder, even now. But I don't think he would have minded. He loved his patients.' She lowered her eyes to her hands. They lay in an unconscious position of prayer on her lap.

'What you must do when people die,' she said, 'is to treat it like an ordinary day. The funeral, too. It must be an ordinary day. You must have the same things for breakfast, and the same things as usual for supper at night. The weather was very ordinary the day Henry was buried. I can't even remember what the sky was like.

The Salvation Army – he'd always supported them – played quieter than I would have liked out in the grave-yard – their form of respect, I suppose, but it was nice. They were completely silent, though, when his coffin was lowered into the grave. They must have misunderstood me. I had said music *all* the time. Anyway. They gave me this handful of earth to throw, and I threw it, and I just said "thank you." I think it must have been out loud, because people looked at me. But that's what I was think-ing, so that's what I felt like saying.' She sighed. 'It was a very ordinary funeral, and a very ordinary death, Henry's. I realise that.'

It was still only midday when Mrs Fox left. I wondered when Joshua would ring. I had his number, but didn't want to disturb him. I would give him till three o'clock.

I wanted him to be here.

The room had become familiar so quickly. The morning after he had carried me in from the bathroom, leaving behind my toothpaste flowers, it was already familiar. Square, white, unadorned. A few shelves of books, a pine rocking chair, a Spanish rug, a carved wooden tree on the chest of drawers – something Joshua had done last week before his work had started up at this pace again. An immemorable room, but I would never forget it. Now, it was the roses on the pelmets in the bedroom in the mews house that were unclear in my mind; the exact placing of the ornaments that were never moved on the fireplace. And I had slept there six years.

The telephone rang. I felt myself smiling.

'Clare? It's David.'

'I'm ill,' I said, making my voice sound worse than it was. 'I can't really talk.'

'Oh, I'm sorry. Anything serious?' He sounded concerned. It was something he and Jonathan had always had in common. Instant concern.

'No, no. Just 'flu.'

'Is there anything you need?'

'No thanks. Just sleep.'

'I won't keep you talking then. Ring me when you feel better.'

I slammed down the receiver. I wanted Joshua to be here.

I had never become used to waiting. When Richard first went to sea I was very bad at it. I would space the days out between the arrival of postcards – he seldom wrote me a letter – and the rare events of a long distance call. There was nothing to do with the days in Portsmouth. It was almost unbearably boring and I disliked the hotel life. I hated eating dinner by myself in the dining-room at seven every evening, barely protected by my book from the fresh young headwaiter. I was intolerant of the young wives who tried to be friendly with their offers of coffee mornings and organised outings to a historical place – to keep their minds alive, as they explained. My lack of enthusiasm soon stopped their offers, and on many days I spoke to no-one but hotel staff.

I wrote to Richard every day. I liked writing letters, and believed he would be interested in my dull news if I could make a good story of the non-events. I told him about how I drove about the countryside in our Anglia, and how petrol had gone up, and how I was trying to teach myself Spanish from one of those do-it-yourself books, and how I'd like a baby, next time he came back. I told him I missed him, but I understood about his career.

Sometimes, though, when I tried to remember him, I

became confused. I had no photographs, and at one time the picture of his face completely eluded me. I panicked. I lay awake night after night willing myself to remember. His backview was clear: the high, bony shoulders, the upright back, the neat line of hair beneath his cap. I made him turn round, slowly, in my mind, but he had no face.

I went down to the harbour one afternoon to re-enact his last departure. There was a ship close by, much like his. I walked to the gangway and stood there, holding the ropes. We had both stood at an identical gangway two months ago, holding a small case between us. He had lowered his head close to mine.

'Good-bye, little one,' he'd said. 'Take care of yourself. I'll send you some chocolates.' Those were always his parting words. He kissed my cheek just below one eye, so lightly that the inner wet part of his lips did not touch me. Then he drew back and looked down at me from his skinny height.

I looked up now, to the width of dappled sky. Funnels, in the distance. Cranes. Two seagulls croaking, humped in slow motion on an invisible wind. Then, at last, the slow recollection of eyes, nose, mouth, the shape of a head with its gold banded cap.

It had worked. I ran back to the town. I ran into a tea shop and ordered home-made brown bread, doughnuts and coffee. I felt myself smiling idiotically at the other customers in their wheelback chairs. I didn't care. I had remembered Richard's face, and there were only three weeks till he came back again.

*

Lunchtime came and went. I sipped very bright orange juice. Still Joshua didn't ring, but the door bell did. A boy

handed me a huge bunch of pink roses, prim and culti-
vated, arrow-pointed buds. Jonathan's mother had
spectacular roses in her garden in Dorset – great shabby
things with dappled petals that darkened towards their
centres. It was in her rose garden, in fact, that he had
proposed to me, one June evening, as we walked one
behind the other, because of the narrowness of the paths,
between the beds of Queen Elizabeth and the Golden
Glory. He had obviously laid his plans for the proposal
most carefully: he had resisted my attempts to take
secateurs and a basket to the garden, and I had had no
suspicions. When I said yes, all right, I would, he had
pulled at a fat scarlet bloom, trying to pluck it for me in
some appropriate symbolic gesture: but he tore the stem
and the petals fell to the ground.

'Never mind,' he said, 'what matters is that now we're
going to be together, together, *together* for the rest of our
lives.' He hitched up his trousers, gave a little skip, and an
instant tear ran from one eye.

*

Joshua had never sent me roses before. I ripped at the
cellophane and slit the envelope to get the small card.
Unmistakably, it was written in a florist's hand. *Clare –
cheer up! Get better soon. Love, David.*

I rammed the roses into the kitchen sink, uncaring,
because there was no vase deep enough to hold their long,
anæmic stems, and no scissors to cut them with. Then I
went back to bed and watched the hands of the clock till
three.

Joshua wasn't at the number he had given me. They
hadn't seen him and didn't know when to expect him.
How to get through the long afternoon?

Find a flat, or a house, that was it. Do something useful. I wouldn't ring agencies, in case Joshua tried to ring me, and he never tried again if a number was engaged. But I could go through the papers. – In one glance, there were an amazing amount of suitable places for us. It would be easy when the time came. The small Georgian terrace house in Kennington, for instance. Joshua liked that side of the river. It would be quiet, and quite convenient. Probably not too good for shopping, but there would be plenty of time to go elsewhere. It would be an unhurried life. Time to read, to learn to cook, to find bargains in junk shops for the house. Even to have a child, perhaps, one day. I would go abroad with Joshua on his filming trips, and we would come back to find a pine grandfather clock still ticking in the hall, and expensive frozen things in the ice box because we could afford to spend a lot of money on food. The house had a small back-garden, it said, with two apple trees. Eating apples, perhaps. We could have windows on to the garden leading from one of those kitchen-dining rooms. It would always be untidy, with an old sofa and telephone books and strings of onions. I would cook breakfast there, go into the garden and pick an apple, and shine it on my *apron*. But perhaps Joshua would like better this studio flat near Ladbroke Grove with a spiral staircase to the bedroom? I marked the paper with huge crosses. My head began to thump.

It was very hot in the room, now. The sky darkened across the window, although it was only four o'clock. Sweat. Damp, scrumpled sheets. Aching throat.

In a studio flat we could begin to collect contemporary pictures. Great bursts of colour on the studio walls. We would change them about. Pictures should be moved. In Jonathan's parents' house the pictures stayed in the same place for so many years that when they were taken down for their annual cleaning, they left black rims on the walls.

Why was there no fresh lemonade with ice? Jonathan made the stuff by the pint. Joshua could only mix Bloody Marys.

My hair was sticking wetly to my head.

Perhaps Joshua could carve something *big* for the studio. He'd never done anything really big.

Where was he?

Hell, I wanted clean sheets, cool pillows, a voice telling me not to make such a fuss. Smooth hands, like Jonathan's, on my head; the reassurance that he wouldn't go away.

Where was Jonathan, now? In his Roman attic, still, with his electric typewriter? Why wasn't he here, comforting?

And then this face grinned at me again, friendly, helpful. He didn't speak, but he carried the basket covered with the white cloth, still, filled with things to make me better.

*

I was being shaken. Jonathan was here at last, rougher than usual, but with lemonade, perhaps, in our big blue jug.

'Jonathan. . . . ?'

'It's not Jonathan. It's me.' Joshua was crouched on the floor by my bed, his head close to mine. 'You're still half asleep. Having bad dreams?' He smiled. 'How are you?' He touched my cheek with his flaky thumb. 'You're burning.' He pushed the hair back from my forehead. 'Speak to me.'

'I've found some nice places to live,' I said. Very slowly, his face tightened into a frown.

'What do you mean?'

'Well, we can't stay here for ever, can we? It's too small.' It hurt to talk.

'I suppose it is,' he said, then he got up. 'Guess what I've brought you? Fresh limes. I thought we could squeeze them. And a bag of hot chestnuts for my supper. You won't be able to eat those, will you? – your throat.' He was funny, somehow. I laughed. Later he came back with a glass of pale green, sweet lime juice, filled with ice. He put it on the table, sank on to the bed, and lay heavily across me, taking my face in his hands.

'I'm sorry,' he said. 'I'm sorry, I'm sorry, I'm sorry.' His mouth closed over my dry lips, his hands began to pull back the bedclothes so that I was suddenly cold.

'Together, together, together . . .' went on a voice. But it was Jonathan who had said that. Joshua was still kissing me.

Chapter Ten

Mrs Fox complained that Joshua, like the friends who had come to her party, had no sense of occasion. She spent Christmas Day with us, her festive spirit battling with his unseasonal one. We ate fried joints of supermarket turkey so that there would be no cold carcass to finish up. We ate frozen peas and baked potatoes and tinned Christmas pudding with brandy butter made by Mrs Fox. In comparison with everything else that, at least, was a triumph.

A pink nylon tree stood on the table, glowing with silver balls spaced mathematically by the manufacturer. Joshua had bought it because, he said, it was the most anti-Christmas symbol he could find. He hated Christmas, but liked not to ignore it. He was good at his discontent, funny. To make up for his apathy he bought us extravagant presents. Mrs Fox had a fur muff and velvet cushions for her bed. For me, Indian jewellery and a set of Victorian prints in beautiful frames.

After lunch we ate the box of crystallised gooseberries Mrs Fox had brought.

'Henry's favourites,' she explained. 'The only ones that didn't get in his teeth.' She was wearing, over her customary black dress, a cardigan made entirely of sequins. They winked and fluttered in the dull electric light. A bunch of goose feathers, dipped in silver paint and dried into hard spikes, was stuck in the band of her hat.

'What are we going to do now?' she asked. 'Christmas

afternoon is always such a problem. I remember, it always was. Edith always came to us for the day, of course, because she never had many social invitations, all her life. Edith never came immediately to people's minds when they planned a party, if you know what I mean. So Henry and I always had her over. We'd have a nice lunch, then Henry'd always be off, in his black coat and carrying his bag, just as if it were a normal day. He wouldn't wait for a call – just go off to a few of his patients who lived on their own, and take them a small present. Some of these, usually, for those who could digest them.' She held up another gooseberry. 'They loved him, Henry's patients, and no wonder.' She looked at us, sitting near her together on the floor, and sighed, smiling.

'So Edith and I were faced with this long afternoon. Well, she wasn't much of a walker, so we couldn't go out. She didn't play cards, or chess, or backgammon or any game. She didn't do tapestry, or sew, or knit. So occupation-wise, if you see what I mean, we had a small problem. Then one year – what, thirty years ago, I suppose? – I hit on this idea. You see Edith always gave me the same present every year – a black fountain pen with a gold nib and a gold rim round the middle. She was funny like that: she always gave people presents that she would have liked to have herself. One of her peculiarities, you could call it. Anyway, she always gave me this beautiful pen – it was much too good ever to wear out in a year, of course, but I couldn't tell her that could I? – and I *knew* what handling a new pen would mean to Edith. So one year I thought to myself, I thought: I'll give Edith writing-paper, and she can spend the afternoon writing her thank-you letters with *my pen*. I found a beautiful box – I'll never forget it, the box I found that first year. It was covered with violets, raised up sort of violets, on the lid, and inside the paper was the palest violet colour you could ever imagine. It even smelt of violets. I don't mean those rubbishy synthetic smells they douse paper with these days. I mean just a trace of woodland violets. Each sheet of paper was stamped with a flower in the corner, and the envelopes were lined with purple tissue paper. Edith was quite taken aback. "Oh my," she said. And I said to her, "Why don't you use it now, Edith? We've got a long afternoon. I could help you with your thank-you letters." "But I don't have my pen with me, Eth," she said. "Ha ha," I said, "perhaps we can find a solution to that." '

Mrs Fox paused in her story and with one hand rubbed over the lumps of ruby and star-sapphire rings on her fingers of the other, as if to warm them.

'So I went over to the big roll-top desk by the fire and cleared a space among the cards on the blotter. Edith laid out the first page and smoothed it very slowly with her hand. She sat down, and I knew she was ready. I picked up my pen and handed it to her. Well, you should have seen her face. "But Eth, it's the pen I've just given you," she said. "Are you sure?" "Of course I am, silly," I said. "I've even got you ink to match." And I took out a bottle of lovely deep purple ink that I'd hidden in a drawer. Edith dipped the clean nib right into the ink, and filled it, and I remember she was trembling. And then the funny thing was, she held it over the paper, and she turned to me and said: "What can I write, Eth?" Well, of course, that was the start of it all. From then on, every year, I dictated her letters on Christmas afternoon while Henry was out. Not that she had many to write. But Miss Turner from the post office always sent her handkerchiefs, and her butcher once sent her a nice crown of lamb, and the woman next door always made her a woolly robin – rubbish, really – in a kind of arrangement which had to be thrown out when the holly died.'

She stopped again, briefly, for breath. Then went on: 'The funny thing about those afternoons was that as soon as we had fallen into this letter-writing habit they never seemed long again. In a jiffy, it felt, Henry would be back out of the snow, laughing at us and asking for tea. I would always put on the kettle, because Edith would be busy sealing up the envelopes. But somehow, after Henry died, we didn't get so many letters written. For one thing, Miss Turner died too, and I couldn't find the quality of writing-paper to give Edith any more.'

She had kept still for the whole story. Now she swivelled round in her chair to look out of the window. Her sequin cardigan flashed and flared again, kingfisher colours. She tapped at the waxy cardboard of the empty gooseberry box with her quick fingers.

'So what are we going to do?' she asked. 'We should go out.'

'We're going,' said Joshua. 'To the country.'

'What do you mean? Where?' He hadn't told me of any plans.

'Annabel Hammond's coming round. She's invited us all to tea with her mother.' He got up, his back to me. 'Near Windsor.'

'Very nice too,' said Mrs Fox. 'Anything but Kent.' Joshua turned to face me and grinned. He picked up one of Mrs Fox's new velvet cushions and flung it at my head.

'It's all right,' he said, 'she's coming with her friend Bruce. So don't look like that.' He turned to Mrs Fox. 'The trouble with Clare is that she's wracked with jealousy. If I tell her I spent a nice day on Brighton Pier with my mother when I was a child, a green flush spreads from her ankles upwards.'

'Stupid,' I said, half smiling.

'If you've never had reason to be jealous, you've never had reason to love,' said Mrs Fox.

'Well, anyway, it'll all be all right this afternoon.' Joshua was pacing the room now, tweaking at things, the balls on the Christmas tree, the dying poinsettias, as he passed them. 'We'll all be together, and Annabel loves Bruce. – At least, he loves her. And we'll have a terrific tea with Mrs Hammond. She's the best cook I know. She'll make Bruce a lovely mother-in-law.'

'As I said,' repeated Mrs Fox, 'Christmas afternoon can be such a problem.'

Annabel and Bruce arrived punctually at three o'clock. Annabel was tall and thin with smooth blonde hair strained back into a bow. She wore a leather coat with silver studs, pale knubbly stockings and fragile walking shoes made of suède. Perfect for Windsor tea.

'I've heard so much about you – hello.' She held out her hand. I took it. It was bony and compact, taut as a frightened bird's wing. 'This is Bruce Winham. Brucey, where are you?' Without releasing me from her look, she folded her arm behind her back and tugged at a huge cable-knit sweater. A small man with hungry sunken eyes twitched eagerly forward. He had a neat black beard that was forced by the height of his polo-neck collar to stick out at right angles, and he wore gym shoes. He grinned at me, his mouth wide with merrily distorted teeth. A friendly, hopeful face. Joshua introduced Mrs Fox. She stood up smartly. Only Bruce shook her hand.

'Why don't we go straight away?' asked Annabel. 'We can take my car. It would be better than yours, if I

131

remember it rightly, wouldn't it, Josh?' She gave him a narrow, knowing smile.

'It's changed since your day,' he said, 'but it's just as uncomfortable. We'll go in yours.'

Annabel swung her efficient look towards Mrs Fox.

'Can we drop your – aunt anywhere on the way?' she asked me. 'Or does she want to come too?' Her tone was uninviting.

'Mrs Fox is a friend,' I said.

'Of course she's coming too,' said Joshua.

'Very well, let's go then.' Annabel clacked her long silver nails against the silver studs of her belt.

Her car was a white Fiat coupé 124. Joshua, Mrs Fox and I sat in the back, Bruce hunched beside Annabel in front. He began rhythmically to tickle the nape of her neck with a prematurely old finger.

'Stop that, Brucey,' she snapped, 'how can I concentrate on driving?' Obediently he stopped. Joshua held my hand.

We sped to Windsor in almost complete silence. There was ragged snow in the fields and barely a car on the road. It was curiously peaceful. Joshua had been truthful about Annabel. For the moment she was no threat.

Mrs Hammond lived up a long laurel hedged drive. Icy puddles spat under the wheels of the car as Annabel screeched round the gentle corners. For a moment Mrs Fox clutched at Joshua's knee. He covered her hand with his, and we jerked to a halt in front of the Tudor house.

It looked warm and comfortable. A garland of holly and scarlet ribbon on the front door. Mullioned windows back-lit by fires and shaded lights indoors. Inside, it was full of labradors, real ones and china ones.

'Typical sort of place,' Mrs Fox whispered to me. 'Henry had patients from these sort of houses. Smart lot.'

Mrs Hammond stood in front of a large open fire waiting to greet us. She was a smaller version of Annabel, equally thin and neat. Her hair, jersey, skirt and shoes were all of a matching blue-grey.

'Darlings!' She welcomed Joshua by curving clinically against his body, and reaching up with her skinny hand to touch, briefly, his face and hair with her diamond-ring fingers. 'You haven't been to see me for so long, my love? Why haven't you been?' Her voice was a whine.

She all but ignored me, but was warm to Mrs Fox. Instantly benevolent, confident in her skill at dealing with other people's odd relations, as she apparently supposed. At the other end of the room Bruce gave a little skip, light on his feet in his gym shoes.

'Lovely thick carpets,' he remarked happily.

'What was that, darling?' Mrs Hammond's whine rose.

'I said: lovely thick carpets.' He skipped over to her. She disapproved of him, but could hardly resist him.

'They are rather nice, aren't they, on a parquet floor?'

Annabel switched in with her organising voice again.

'Why don't we all go out before it's dark? I feel like some exercise. Anyone else? Brucey? Josh?'

'We'll all come,' said Joshua.

Except Mrs Hammond, we all went. Annabel, in spotless gum-boots now, led the way through the misty garden. We followed her through a small gate into a ploughed field. Here, the hard black earth split through the old snow, leaving it to lie in frozen white snakes between the ridges. We began to walk single file round the edges of the field. The hedges, wet with cobwebs, scratched at our sides.

Suddenly Joshua, who was in front of me, stopped. He bent down and scooped up a handful of the icy snow. Then

133

he jumped at me and rubbed it quickly over my cheeks. It stung.

'You dare!'

'Catch me, then.' I flung out my arms, but he had gone. Leaping over the plough.

'I will.' I sprang after him. I was aware of the other three, behind me, stopping and turning to watch. I chased him to the middle of the field, half-running, half-jumping from furrow to furrow. It was heavy going. The solid wet earth clung to my feet.

'You'll never get me!' He stopped for a moment, panting, his face alight and excited.

'I will.' With mock ferocity I now made a snowball, picking up lumps of earth with the snow, in my haste, and threw it hard at him. He ducked, and it missed. He laughed.

'Bad luck, Funny Face. It's the aim that counts, you see. Look, like this.' Quickly he made another snowball and leapt up, stretching his whole body, to fling it at me with all his apparent force. This time I turned my head to duck and dodge it, imitating his speed. I took a step backwards at the same time, tripped over a hard ridge of earth, and fell. I fell in the middle of a furrow, knees apart, hands askew beneath me. Icy bits of snow stung through my tights, and I felt the black earth push up behind my nails. Joshua was still laughing.

'Are you all right?' He came over to me, unconcerned.

'I think so.' He helped me up and brushed snow and earth from my coat.

'You're not much good, are you? Here, you've got mud on your face, too. How did that happen?' He scraped it away with hard cold fingers. 'Now you look marvellous.'

'Don't be funny,' I said.

'No, really, I mean it. Your cheeks are bright pink, for once, and your eyes are shining quite ridiculously.'

'And I suppose you'd rather have me with mud on my coat and an undignified mess than the immaculate Annabel?' I asked, tightly.

'Yes,' he said. He held my hand. It was cold, but warmer than mine.

We began to walk heavily back over the plough to the hedge. The others, equally spaced, stood where we had left them, watching our progress in silence. Mrs Fox stood to attention, her new fur muff hanging from a black satin ribbon round her neck, her hands clenched at her sides. Beneath the black sleeves of her coat hung small sparkling rims of cardigan, flashing silver and white now as the sequins reflected the scattered snow. She looked very serious.

Annabel spoke first, as soon as we were in earshot.

'That was very amusing,' she said. 'You always were so energetic, Josh.'

'I think we better go back to the house,' said Joshua, coldly. 'Clare should get cleaned up.'

'Oh heavens. Is it that serious? Surely no-one minds a bit of mud. I mean, we've only just started.' Annabel stamped her foot. Her nostrils flared.

'She's pretty wet,' said Joshua.

'For myself,' said Mrs Fox, 'I'm going back to the garden. I want to take a look in the greenhouse we passed. If that's all right with you, of course, Miss Hammond?'

'Of course,' said Annabel. Having made her successful interruption, Mrs Fox thrust both her hands disapprovingly into her muff, and turned to plod back down the field towards the garden gate. The rest of us watched her go without speaking. Eventually her small, upright figure disappeared through the gate.

'I'll go back to the house on my own,' I said. 'You all go on.'

'That's the solution,' said Annabel, 'if you don't mind.' Joshua looked from her to me.

'Shall we do that?' He seemed not to mind which way the problem was settled.

'Sure.' I turned to go. Annabel suddenly smiled, her lips two thin slithers of silvery grease.

'We won't be long, anyway,' she said. 'Mother will show you round in the house.'

Then, spontaneously, Bruce took my arm.

'I tell you what, *I'll* go with Clare. Come on, Clare. Don't let's dither any more. I'm getting cold.' He was shivering. Joshua and Annabel turned the other way. We parted.

Almost at once Bruce was forced to walk behind me because of the narrowness of the path.

'Bloody damp,' he said, after a while. 'I loathe the bloody country.'

The sky was full of deepening shades now, grey and pink, turtle-dove colours. Against it, winter trees stood with tousled heads of hair on skinny necks, and pigeons flew towards the same wood that Joshua and Annabel were heading for.

By the time we reached the garden gate the daylight had closed down almost to darkness. In the silence, cinder paths between navy-blue hedges scrunched under our muddy feet.

'Let's join Mrs Fox in the greenhouse,' Bruce said, bouncing amiably to my side again. 'I can't face too long with Mrs Hammond without Annabel's protection.'

We made our way to the greenhouse, but Mrs Fox had left. Bruce turned the rusty key and we went in. It was warm and damp and neat. Shelves of poinsettias, cyclamens and azaleas, searing red and mushy pink in the feeble electric light. Bruce ran his hand along a rusty pipe bound up with rusty rags.

'She sells them, as you can imagine,' he said, indicating the flowers. 'She's the sort of woman who would put six tame chickens into a battery unit if she thought she could make a profit out of them that way.' I laughed, feeling warmer at last. He sat on the pipe, now, testing it carefully first, and looked up at me. 'So now it's you and Joshua?'

'How do you mean?'

'Annabel told me he was nuts about someone.'

'I don't think he is.'

'It still hurts her, you know. She pretends it doesn't, but I know bloody well it does. She was crazy about him for three years. Nervous breakdowns, the lot.'

I turned from him to prod the warm, feathery earth in a small pot of cacti.

'What are you?' I asked.

'Film industry. What else? Totally unsuccessful, of course, and with little potential. Just striving, hoping, as they say. But I'm quite a pleasant fellow to have around on any set, so I get the jobs, and who cares about the prestige?'

'How long have you known Joshua?'

'Oh, years. I can't remember when I first met him. I've always admired him and, to be honest, I suppose I've tried to model myself on him. But I've always been the utility model. What I can never achieve is his – distance, shall I call it? There I am, grinning away, showing

137

exactly what's going on in my mind, while he switches into this beautiful – distance.' He grinned. 'You can never tell what Joshua's thinking. That's what I admire. The enigma. The apparent lack of concern – then all of a sudden he surprises you. Like, when I was in hospital once for a long time, he didn't make any promises to come and see me, like everyone else. But unlike everyone else he just came, every day. Bloody miles out of London it was, too. And I don't mean that much to him.

'Funny thing is, I've done a lot of the same things as Joshua – only some years later. Including Annabel, of course.' He laughed, amused at himself. 'Naturally, I'm nothing like Joshua was to her. But at least I offer her security, which is more than he ever did. Her mother can hardly abide me, as you can imagine, what with my lack of what she calls "background", and that. But still, probably she won't marry me in the end, so Mrs Hammond will be no problem.'

I wondered how Joshua had treated Annabel.

'Like a bastard,' replied Bruce crossly. 'Really dreadful. Always letting her down, getting at her, threatening her. He had the upper hand completely. Of course,' he sighed, 'he was right. That's what she responds to best, and that's what I just can't do. I *can't* treat her like that, not loving her like this. In fact there's only one way I know I really can please her, and that won't last for ever, will it?'

He stood up. We were exactly the same height.

'So now you're going through it all? I wonder how you're making out?'

'Who can tell?' I asked. 'I can't.'

'Well, as long as Joshua can't tell what effect he's having on you, you'll keep him. That's where Annabel went wrong. He was bored stiff as soon as she began declaring her love. He's a terrible child like that. Win the chase, and the game is over for him, no matter how good the prize.'

We left the greenhouse and he locked the door again.

'If you ask me, you're doing pretty well,' he said. 'You've got him in pretty good shape.'

'I hope so,' I said. It was quite dark in the garden now. The lights from the house flickered through a tangle of silhouette bushes. Bruce took my arm and led me to the path.

'If ever I can help,' he said.

*

Back in the drawing-room Mrs Hammond and Mrs Fox sat in opposite arm-chairs by the fire. Mrs Fox had a pile of magazines dumped on her knee. Mrs Hammond had probably put them there, saying 'Something to read,' like a doctor's receptionist, not caring how unsuitable they were as long as they kept Mrs Fox quiet. Mrs Hammond herself dabbed expertly at a piece of *petit point*. Her spiky diamond fingers made small rhythmic jumping movements that flashed with flames from the fire. A table with a white cloth and fragile plates covered with silver lids was laid by the sofa.

'Oh, there you are,' said Mrs Hammond, raising her blue eyes to us above her pale blue sewing glasses. 'I was beginning to wonder what had happened to you.'

'Clare fell over and we had to get her clean,' said Bruce. 'The trouble is, there are so many bathrooms in this house it took quite a time deciding which one to use.'

'*Bruce*, your bitter little jokes,' said Mrs Hammond. 'It's Christmas Day, don't forget. Well, shall we start without them?'

Mrs Fox thankfully removed the pile of magazines from her lap to the floor.

'I could do with a nice piece of Christmas cake,' she said. 'That's one thing we always did away with, Christmas cake. Edith couldn't manage the icing, what with her teeth, and Henry was allergic to marzipan.'

'What's that?' asked Mrs Hammond.

At that moment Joshua and Annabel came through the door. Joshua rubbing his hands, Annabel with noticeably shining hair that looked as if it had been brushed extra hard to disguise previous dishevelment.

'Sorry we're late,' she said, 'you should have started. God, what you missed, though. It was so beautiful in the woods, you can't imagine.' She looked at me, elated. I felt my face red from the fire. 'You should have come, in spite of the mud.'

'What was so beautiful?' asked Mrs Fox.

'What?' Annabel ran her hand impatiently through her hair.

'I said: what was so beautiful in the woods?' repeated Mrs Fox.

'How do you mean?' said Annabel.

'I mean exactly what I say,' said Mrs Fox.

For a moment there was puzzled silence in the room. No-one cared to help. I glanced at the loud ticking clock. Ten past five. We could leave at six. Annabel drew a chair up to the table and sat down. She motioned to Joshua to sit beside her.

'For heaven's sake! Am I being that inarticulate? Perhaps you're not a country lover. Perhaps you only like towns in winter . . .' Her voice was feeble. She was put out.

'Not at all,' said Mrs Fox, and gave me a small, private smile.

The rest of us joined Annabel at the table. Mrs Hammond, with a flicker of new respect, poured Mrs Fox the first cup of tea. We ate crumpets and banana sandwiches. The huge Christmas cake was decorated with icing-sugar hills. Small plaster figures ski-ed down the slopes and nylon fir trees were dotted in the valleys. Mrs Fox laughed with delight.

'Have you ever seen anything like it?' she asked Bruce.

'Never,' he said, 'dreadfully vulgar, isn't it?' Annabel and Joshua both laughed at the same time. 'When I was a child my mother would buy a slab of Dundee cake at Christmas time and spread on a thin bit of icing herself. We thought *that* was lovely.'

'Really, Bruce, you're always trying to shock me,' said Mrs Hammond.

'We must all *play* something after tea,' said Annabel. 'Wouldn't that be a good idea?'

'I think we really ought to be getting back,' I said.

'What on earth *for*? You can't be that engaged on Christmas night. You're either *doing* something *positive*, or you're not.' I looked at Joshua.

'I'm in no particular hurry,' he said. 'What about you, Mrs Fox?' Mrs Fox was trying to unstick a fir tree from her huge slice of cake.

'Can I keep it?' she asked, as it broke away, a heavy chunk of icing clinging to its roots.

'Of course,' said Mrs Hammond, 'and if you all agree to stay to dinner we'll have my special soufflé that comes in on fire.' She smiled conspiratorially at her daughter.

'In that case we should stay, shouldn't we?' Mrs Fox asked Joshua. 'We couldn't miss that. In my day,' she explained to Mrs Hammond, 'I was quite a gourmet. It was all because Henry's patients would come to me to try out their little experiments.' The fir tree and the thought of a fiery pudding had won over Mrs Fox. Her noble stand against the Hammonds was weakened, and she had them in her control now. Annabel, triumphant, encouraged her to tell stories. Mrs Fox took her cue, performed, and was well received.

'*Such* a beautiful cardigan, that, Mrs Fox,' said Annabel at one moment. In the firelight its icy coloured sequins sparkled with gold; fulgid, alive, reflecting dancing patterns on her face.

'You exaggerate,' said Mrs Fox, 'it's just an old thing I got at a jumble sale.' Bruce turned wickedly to Annabel.

'What do you mean by beautiful?' he asked.

'For heaven's sake!' She screeched with laughter.

'You'll learn to laugh *with* people one day, you patronising bitch,' he said quietly, so that Mrs Fox shouldn't hear.

After tea he and I played Scrabble while the other four played bridge.

'I'm sorry you weren't able to get away,' he said. 'Dinner will doubtless be the kind of merry occasion you wouldn't have minded missing. Mrs Hammond likes her champagne.'

A white-coated Spanish butler appeared with the first bottle at six-thirty. Mrs Hammond broke up the game of bridge to take a glass with her to the kitchen. Annabel went up for a bath.

'I can't lend you anything for dinner, I suppose?' she said, before she left. 'We're not exactly the same size, are we?'

'She's a great one for always making her point,' said Bruce, when she had left.

'She hasn't changed,' said Joshua. He came and sat

down on the low fire stool. 'You seem to be casting a certain gloom.'

'I'm not feeling my gayest.'

'There's nothing to worry about, idiot.' It was then, in the light of the fire, that I saw a miniscule speck of silver grease glinting on his chin. I took my handkerchief and wiped it off.

'Silver shines,' I said. I paused, fighting not to say it. I lost. 'It *must* have been beautiful in the woods.' For a moment Joshua stiffened, then he smiled. Bruce watched him carefully.

'She pounced on me like a tiger,' he said.

'The bitch. Christ, the bitch.' Bruce winced. 'It was only after lunch, just before we came round to meet you. . . .'

'I'm sorry Bruce. But anyway, she didn't succeed.' Joshua put his hand on my knee. Bruce untied the laces of one of his gym shoes then re-tied it, more tightly, with a fierce tug.

'My trouble is, I love the girl,' he said. 'I love her with a ludicrous passion that doesn't get either of us anywhere. I know my role. Unfortunately, I can't seem to stop playing it.'

Annabel reappeared an hour later. She wore a magnificent gold trouser suit whose top was unzipped to just below her breasts. Plainly she wore no bra beneath.

'Wow,' said Bruce, sadly.

'Fantastic,' said Joshua. They both rose to fill her glass. She laughed at their attention.

'Isn't this fun?' she asked me.

'Great fun,' I said. My cardigan felt enormous and hot. My feet blazed in my thick boots. My head ached from the heat and champagne.

At eight o'clock a gong was rung. Dinner was served. We filed in like two badly matched teams; Mrs Hammond, Annabel and Mrs Fox dressed for the occasion; Bruce, Joshua and I decidedly out of place in the claustrophobic, red dining-room. The mahogany table was laid with a clutter of candles and crackers, dazzling silver and glass, and a dreadful winter-scene centrepiece with a mirror lake, cotton-wool snow and more nylon fir trees. Jonathan would have loved it.

Soup, first. Mulberry coloured stuff thick with *croutons*.

'What an amusing little soup,' said Bruce, to break the warm silence.

'*Bruce*, I never know whether to take you seriously or not,' said Mrs Hammond. Her cheeks were flushed to the same colour as the soup. 'The funny thing about me is, I never know whether someone is complimenting me or insulting me.'

'That is a happy confusion in which you should always remain,' replied Bruce.

'What a lovely centrepiece!' Mrs Fox left her soup to prod the cotton-wool snow with a finger. 'Did you make it, Mrs Hammond?'

'Of course. Everything in this house is home-made that can be home-made. I've always been very good with my hands.'

'And does Annabel take after you?' The old sharpness had returned to Mrs Fox's voice. Bruce answered her.

'She's marvellous with her hands,' he said. Joshua spluttered into his soup. Annabel glanced at him through half-shut fake lashes.

'What do you say to that, Josh?' Joshua looked from Bruce to her.

'Oh, marvellous,' he said lightly. 'Anything you undertake to do, you do well.' Everyone but me laughed. Mrs Hammond joined in the spirit of the joke.

'I don't know what Joshua and Bruce can know about it,' she said, 'I swear they've never caught her knitting, or arranging flowers or anything. How can you judge?'

'We can judge,' said Joshua.

I pushed my soup away, sickened. Annabel noticed immediately.

'Anything the matter, Clare?'

'No.'

'You must be dreadfully hot in that cardigan.'

'I am, rather.'

'Poor you. We can't open the window, either. There's something wrong with the sash.' I felt a hot icicle of sweat trickle down my spine. The candle flames wavered and fattened before my eyes. I removed my hand from where it had lain slumped on the table. Five misted-up fingermarks remained on the shining surface. 'It's ghastly, suffering from heat,' Annabel went on. 'I feel so sorry for people who do. I love it, myself. Crazy about the sun, aren't I Josh? Do you remember? St Tropez? I'm quite happy just to *lie*. Just to lie in the sun for hours, doing nothing but getting brown. I suppose it's awfully *boring*, really, for anyone who's with me. Wasn't it, Josh?'

'Fairly,' said Joshua. They smiled at each other, acknowledging the lie. Something grated behind my eyes. On Christmas night last year, Jonathan, in his shiny old dinner jacket, had said I was beautiful. His mother's dining-room had been uncomfortably hot, too. But he had noticed my unease halfway through the smoked salmon. Without saying anything he had opened the door and make a chink in the heavy curtains. He had cared.

Joshua was warming to Annabel's reminiscences. He

145

sat with his fork suspended over his plate of left-over turkey disguised in a spicy sauce, his face hard-cut shadows and planes in the candlelight, his eyes restless behind the massive frames of his glasses, his mouth up-turned on one side only as he smiled – beautiful.

Joshua – get up from the table now, come over to me, take my hand, and tell everybody we are leaving. . . .

'Annabel is such a sophisticated traveller,' Joshua was saying. 'Wherever you go she knows about the most interesting church, the best local wine, the cheapest good restaurant, don't you? And then she's always changing, aren't you? Three or four times a day as far as I could make out. She manages to produce endless clothes and yet a very small amount of luggage. I could never understand it.'

'Quite,' snapped Bruce.

Let's go right now, please Joshua. Out into the night, quickly to the airport. Let's catch a plane to anywhere, anywhere as long as it's away from these people. And let's tell them why we're leaving.

The promised soufflé came, swaying pale and high above its dish, blue brandy flames lapping up its sides. Mrs Fox clapped her hands.

You could buy two of those miniature bottles of brandy, and we could ask the air-hostess for a rug. . . .

I looked at Joshua, but his eyes flicked away, back to Annabel. She was flushed now, not an ugly red flush with hard edges, as I felt my own to be, but the natural colour of her cheeks was intensified just enough to make her hard eyes bluer. She was excited, beautiful, prepared to make her next move, any move, so long as Joshua kept reacting.

'But my darling Josh,' she said, '*you* are such a child on

holiday. Remember? Remember how you always used to be running away from me in foreign towns, playing childish games. I could never speak the *language*, that was my problem, so I could never ask if anyone'd seen you.' Joshua paused in the middle of helping himself to the soufflé.

'You exaggerate,' he said, no longer smiling. On my own plate the flames fizzled out round a fiery mound of fluff. I held on to the solid mahogany underbelly of the table.

'I exaggerate? Absolute nonsense.' So concerned was she with her own pace, that Annabel was unaware now that Joshua had fallen behind her. 'Don't say you've forgotten that time – where was it? God knows, England somewhere, I think – that time you ran off for *hours* leaving me on some God-forsaken beach. And when at last you came back you didn't care a damn that I was *perished*. You were very pleased with yourself, in fact, because you'd managed to get us *ice creams*, two bloody choc bars if I remember – '

'Shut up, Annabel!' My scream ripped into her. She stopped. In silence, everyone looked at me. I trembled, I burned. 'You reminiscing bitch. What are you trying to do?'

'What have I done?' Her voice cool, concealing a smile. Her head tipped up towards me now, innocently. Then all the heads tipped up, so that shadowy cheeks suddenly flared with gold light from the candles. I was standing. I looked at Joshua and the others faded.

'Come on,' I said. 'Come on, let's go.' Pause. No answer. He still held my eyes. 'Quickly. Please. It's time for us to go.' He got up, came to my chair and pulled it away, freeing me from the trap between it and the table.

Then he went to the door, opened it for me, and gestured to me to go through. He didn't follow. I turned round to wait for him. He was shutting the door.

'That was a pretty scene,' he said, so quietly I could hardly hear, and the door closed.

I began to run through corridors – close-carpeted, hunting scenes on the walls, dimpled light from chandeliers. I chose a door with an ornate brass handle. An unused room, cold. Very high leather chairs. Grey walls, guns, a stuffed labrador in a glass cage, a steel-framed photograph of a man with Annabel's eyes, one of them was widened behind a monocle. Leather arm-chair very cold behind my knees, very cold arms under my hands. Directly opposite my chair the labrador, its flinty pink tongue painless on icicle teeth, smiled its dead smile.

*

About half an hour later there was a tap on the door. I didn't answer. Mrs Fox came in.

'Heavens, child, you'll catch your death in here,' she said, going to the small electric fire that stood dwarfed at the foot of the huge fireplace. She switched on its two thin bars. 'Typical meanness of these sort of people. Henry was always having to go to people who'd caught pneumonia by economising on the central heating when they needn't have. They'd cut out a radiator here, a radiator there, just to prove to themselves they weren't extravagant. But then the rich have some funny illusions about cutting down, don't they?' She went over to the dog and tapped at the glass case, her back to me. 'What an awful creature! Joshua said I should tell you we will be leaving shortly. I wouldn't have liked to have a dog like that alive, let alone dead.'

She turned to me. In this room her sequined cardigan glittered deep violet, navy, and dull silver, subdued. She still wore her black hat with its silver painted goose feathers and, as usual, one hand rubbed at the lumpy rings on the other.

'They put on Stravinsky in the drawing-room when we went through,' she said. 'Well, I thought, if you start listening to *that*, you'll never leave. So I thought I'd come and find you. Joshua saw me going and gave me the message.'

'Mrs Fox,' I said.

'That's all right,' she said. She went now to the huge desk in the corner. It had a carved roll-top which she fingered gently. 'Very like ours,' she said, 'very like ours. I mean, like the one I was telling you about where Edith used to write her Christmas letters. Do you think anyone would mind – ?' Gently she pushed up the lid. Underneath, polished brass handles shone on a pattern of small drawers. There were no papers, no pens, no ink. Mrs Fox was disappointed. 'It's all deserted,' she said, pulling back the lid. 'I've never liked an empty desk.'

Through the door came the distant sound of Joshua calling us. I didn't move.

'Come along now, up off that chair.' Mrs Fox spoke with the same voice she had used to Edith on the park bench. 'We must go, and about time too.' Still I didn't move. Mrs Fox moved slowly towards me. She seemed to sag a little. 'Come along, please.' She put out her hand, the one with the rings, so that they flashed like a morse code back at her sequined sleeve. 'Take my arm, if you would. You'd never believe it, but I'm a little tired.' It didn't matter whether or not she spoke the truth. I got up, and took her arm. The sequins felt splintery under my hand. We walked past the smiling dog and out into the passage.

'I didn't turn the fire off on purpose, of course,' said Mrs Fox, 'it just might make that little difference to Mrs Hammond's bill, mightn't it?'

We turned the corner. At the far end of the passage, in the brightly lit hall, the Hammonds, Joshua and Bruce, unaware of us, were talking and laughing round the Christmas tree, pulling on coats, kissing Mrs Hammond, saying they'd love to come again; saying, yes, really, it had been a lovely time, a lovely Christmas Day.

Chapter Eleven

'There's something about your quietness,' said Richard Storm, 'that never bores me.' We were driving along country lanes looking for another cottage which Richard didn't want to see, but had agreed to for my sake. It was a Saturday morning. Spring. Primroses on the steep banks of the lanes. A hotel picnic, or 'wrapped lunch' as they called it, in a basket on the back seat. A day full of anticipation, full of promise. But weighing against it, a familiar heaviness of limb: a solidity of heart where there should have been lightness. But never mind. Excitement, when we found the cottage, was just round the corner.

'No, I can never understand it. It never ceases to puzzle me.' Richard was talking quietly, almost to himself. He steered our light Anglia with heavy solemnity, as if he guided a huge ship. 'When I'm away at sea, I picture you sometimes – '

'Oh, you think of me?' I smiled at him. He looked back seriously.

'Of course. What do you imagine? You're my wife, aren't you? Sailors think of their wives when they're away at sea.'

'I wasn't being very serious.' He was never a receptive person to joke with.

'Well, I was. I think of you often. I think of you as my child wife, far away from me, waiting for me, and it makes me sad.' He paused.

'What does?'

'Mostly, that we're wasting time. Not just wasting time by being apart, but that I'm wasting time when I could be – educating you.'

'When you could be what?' He coughed, and steered elaborately round a gentle corner.

'Perhaps I haven't chosen the right word. But you know what I mean. You know what I said I'd always do – I'd make my child bride grow up. As I've always said' – now it was his turn to joke, his small mouth cracked appropriately – 'you're good potential material.' A long pause.

'How am I coming on?' I asked. He didn't seem to notice anything about my voice.

'You've come on a lot, in just a year, but the hard way, I'm afraid. Waiting about in hotel rooms for your elderly husband has inevitably matured you, but we've a long way to go, haven't we?' He patted my knee. 'Now don't look offended. You want me to tell you my fantasies, don't you? You've never minded before.'

'I don't mind now. What fantasies?'

'Well, you know, my ridiculous dreams. My old man's dreams, if you like.'

'You're not *that* old. What are these dreams?' A few dots of sweat had gathered on his aquiline nose, and he licked his lips. Under the thin grey flannel of his sporting trousers I could see the muscles of his scraggy thighs gather and tighten.

'Oh, what do they matter on a lovely morning like this? I'll tell you some other time. We've only about a mile to go.'

The cottage, once pretty, now dirty and decaying, stood in an acre of garden over-run with briar roses and apple trees. There was a rotting chicken house at one end of a small orchard, and mushrooms in the grass.

'It's lovely,' I said to Richard. His eyes narrowed as if to scan a far off horizon, although he stood only a few yards from the cottage.

'Hardly lovely,' he said. 'Totally impractical. Miles from anywhere. It would need a fortune spending on it.'

'We haven't looked, yet.'

'A fortune, I can tell you.'

'It might not. Anyway, it's good potential material.' He didn't smile.

'You're childishly stubborn when you want something.' He looked at his watch. 'It's two, already. Let's eat first, then look. Not that looking will take long. It can't be more than two up and two down, whatever the agents say.'

I fetched the basket from the car.

'Let's eat in the garden,' I suggested.

'It's much too chilly, and there's nowhere to sit.'

'On top of the chicken house?'

'And I wouldn't be surprised to find a wind getting up. It's only April, after all.'

'I know you know about winds,' I said, 'but I think it's lovely and warm, the sun.' He didn't hear me, but walked impatiently towards the tattered front door. I followed him.

Inside, bulging walls were streaked with damp, and a pool of water from some old shower had leaked through the window onto the red tiled floor. A smell of rotten apples.

'Marvellous,' said Richard, crossly. 'So much you could do with it for ten thousand pounds.'

'I like it,' I said, 'and I'm the one who would have to be here most.'

'Perhaps,' he said, 'soon I will arrange not to be away so much.'

'Good,' I said. 'Really?'

After one egg sandwich he had rejected a fishpaste sandwich, a chocolate biscuit and a Swiss roll, and now he hungrily ate an apple. We sat on the only piece of furniture, an old chest, mildewed at the sides, with the food spread between us on a paper napkin.

'It could be so nice,' I said. 'Imagine: I would be cooking your breakfast at this window. Birds on the lawn outside. Roses – .'

'I can't imagine,' he said. With every bite of the apple his own Adam's apple jerked up and down, in and out of the slot made by the crisp white collar of his open shirt, which in turn fitted into the V neck of his blue jersey, all the pieces fitting into each other like a puzzle. His thin, neat hair shone, still dented by the cap which for once he wasn't wearing. In mufti Richard looked naked, ill at ease. 'There's one thing,' he said, looking at the damp, 'my child bride will never be able to provide me with, no matter what I do.' The sweat had returned to his forehead.

'What's that?' He turned to me and ran a finger from my shoulder down to my waist.

'I've always liked big breasts.'

'I'm sorry about that.' I laughed. He got up and went to the corner of the room. Tested the wall with the flat of his hand.

'Mushy. Come here. Feel.'

I went over to him and put my hand near his. He took me in his arms and crushed his mouth down on to mine. Peppermint and apple breath. Briefly I struggled.

'What are you doing?'

'What do you think, little one? You're my wife, aren't you?' His bony thighs jiggled against mine. His hand ran up my jersey. 'Will you ever have big breasts for me? Will you?' His voice was breathless.

'Of course not.' I pulled back my head to look at him. There were white spots like cuckoo spit at each corner of his mouth. He grabbed at my waist, screwing my jersey in his hand as it if were loose wool.

'But you could – pull in your waist a little, couldn't you? Wear clothes that show you off more. Eat more and put a little weight on your bottom, couldn't you? Couldn't you?' He panted slightly. One of his claw hands circled round and round my back. 'You could wear more on your face. Your eyes. I like lipstick – .'

'What's the *matter* with you, Richard?' I heard my voice from a long way off, trying to be gay.

'What's the matter, little one? Nothing's the matter except that I want you. And do you know what? I'll want you even more in a few years time, when you're riper, fuller. . . .' His face crushed down on to mine again. His hand hurt in my back. I began to cry. Immediately he let go of me and stepped back. 'Now what's up?' Impatient rather than concerned.

'Nothing. I mean, you frightened me.'

He sighed. So tall, so neat, so pale. His white collar hadn't moved even in the scuffle. A man with sea charts in his head and horizons in his eyes. My stranger husband.

'I'm sorry,' he said, 'but I suddenly wanted you very much. Don't you want me?' A long pause.

'No, not just now,' I said.

'Very well, then, we'll go.' His hands moved almost imperceptibly at his sides, just scuffing his trousers. I put my hand on his arm and felt it stiffen.

155

'I'm sorry,' I said. 'I don't seem to be what you want. You seem to be stimulated by the thought of older women. Is that what you think of when you're making love to me?'

'Of course,' he said. Then he touched my hair quite gently. 'Men have their passions, little one, and a woman's job is to welcome them. But you have a lot to learn.' He began to pick up the picnic things, humming to himself, 'Lady of Spain'.

With me, that was the nearest Richard Storm ever came to passion, and it was the last cottage we ever saw.

*

'You realise it's January, I suppose? Time's nearly up.' David Roberts on the telephone again. 'Have you decided anything? What you're going to do?'

'No.'

'Hadn't you better be making up your mind?'

'There's time,' I said. It was only eight thirty, still dark outside, but Joshua had left at six this morning. Hadn't said why. He was out so much now. Working very hard sorting things out before going to Mexico next month. Mexico.

'I suppose I'd sound like a sentimental old fool if I said I can't help imagining a lovely homecoming,' he said.

'Yes,' I said.

'You're pessimistic about the chances of a happy ending, then?'

'Not pessimistic. Not anything.'

'At the risk of interfering, I think you ought to *think*, soon. Make a positive decision one way or another.'

'There's *time*,' I repeated.

'Not much.' David coughed. 'Anyway, old thing, as an

old friend, I think there's something I ought to tell you –
you ought to know.' He paused, coughed again. 'He'll
never marry you.'

'What do you mean?'

'Joshua.'

'Why do you assume I want to marry him?'

'In the end, like most other women, you'll want to
settle for that sort of security.'

'You might think,' I said, 'that after two marriages
I might not feel inclined to that sort of security any
more.'

'You might, but I don't. – But anyway. Don't take any
notice of me. Who am I to advise? I just don't want you
to say I didn't warn you. Joshua does not marry people,
I'm telling you. Usually, he doesn't love them, either.'

'Thank you for the warning,' I said.

He forced a laugh.

'By Christ, is there anything more touchy than a
separated woman? I don't know why I bother to go on
ringing you. I'm only trying to help, you know.'

'I know, I know.'

'So perhaps it would help to tell you that I have in fact
spoken to Jonathan lately?'

'Oh.'

'And he sounded much more cheerful. Resigned to the
situation, at last, you might say. Very friendly about you.
He asked how you were, what you were doing and so on.
I told him you were getting on fine, without giving
anything away.'

'That was nice of you.'

'He sounded – maybe I got this wrong, we only spoke
on the telephone – but he sounded as if he was *looking
forward* to February. That's what gave me hope. That's

what got the old imagination going, if you know what I mean.'

'Quite.'

'So that's all the news, really. I just wondered how you are, and if you had made the big decision. And I thought you'd be pleased to hear about Jonathan's change of heart, as I know you couldn't want him to be positively unhappy, could you? I mean, hell, he may have his faults. But he's the heck of a *loving* man, isn't he? Which is more than you can say for Joshua. . . .'

*

'Oh, I'm happy, happy, happy,' said Jonathan, 'aren't you, Suki Soo?' This was his name for me at moments of supreme happiness.

We lunched at the hotel, restricted by our *demi-pension* terms, at the balcony restaurant under a striped awning. Jonathan was grateful for the shade. In his determination to stay by my side he had refused, that morning on the beach, to allow himself the protection of the parasol. Instead, he had spent an agonising couple of hours on the glaring white sand. The sun shrank and burned his pale skin, and frizzled up the many oils he dabbed himself with continually. Now, sweat bubbled over his scarlet face and his hair hung in damp peaks under his small straw hat. He looked down on to the beach below us, crowded with browning sunbathers.

'There's something about the Italians, isn't there?' he said. 'I don't know why, but I've always felt something very special towards the I-ties.' He helped himself to a couple of strips of green pepper from the plate of *hors-d'oeuvres*. As he leant forward, his cotton shirt strained over his chest and a button flew off. He didn't notice. 'I wonder

158

what it is? So many Englishmen – creative Englishmen, that is – seem to have it in common. I suppose I'm smitten with the same bug as Keats and Shelley and Lord Byron. I have whatever they had – in that respect.' He bent down to scratch, under the table, the dry skin of one of his legs.

Lunch over, we went to our air-conditioned room because Jonathan, like Shelley, felt he was capable of some of his best work in Italy. His typewriter and papers were spread over the dressing-table. In a week he had typed a couple of pages, the 'outline' for some new play.

I drew the shutters, so that slits of sun and shadow patterned the tiled floor, and lay on the bed. I shut my eyes. I could hear Jonathan sit down at the dressing-table, light a cigarette, search about for an ashtray, shuffle a few papers. Silence for a moment, followed by seven slow thumps on the keyboard. Then the squeal of his chair being pushed back over the tiles.

'Darling? Could you help me a moment? I need your advice. I want to try out something on you.' I opened my eyes. He sat towards me now, legs apart, shorts riding high up his thighs, the curly black hair thickening towards his crutch. His tinted spectacles had slipped down over his nose which even in this light was a sore pink. He re-arranged the few papers in his hands, as if the new arrangement was enormously complicated.

'The thing is, about this kind of outline, it brings the whole thing to life if you throw in a few lines of dialogue to show them the sort of thing they can expect in the final script. Well, how about this for the start of Scene Two?' He cleared his throat.

' "*Scene: the kitchen of a large, comfortable farm house.*" ' He looked up and smiled. 'I hope you note, darling, that I'm

159

not writing a drawing-room comedy. Far from it. Anyway, as I say, the large, comfortable kitchen of a farm house – or the other way round, as I think I said before. What does it matter? ' "*A middle-aged couple and a young couple are sitting at a table eating soup. There is silence, except for the supping*" – good word, that for soup, isn't it? – "*except for the supping of the soup, then suddenly the oldest man, Thomas, stands up.*

THOMAS: *My God, Marcia! My God! Say something, can't you? How can you carry on eating your soup like that?*" '

'Jonathan scraped his chair a few inches nearer to the bed and raised his eyebrows in preparation for Marcia's high voice.

' "MARCIA: *Sit down and get on with your soup, Horace. It's lovely soup. It'll get cold if you don't get on with it.*

THOMAS: *How can you all think about soup at a moment like this?*

MARCIA: *Come on, Horace, it's your favourite, isn't it? Carrot and onion. I did it specially for you –* " '

Jonathan turned, slammed the papers back on the dressing-table, then swivelled back to me again.

'You see the kind of thing I'm trying to do? Here's this fat, insensitive man, Horace, in a rage, and the only reaction he can get from his wife Marcia is comments on the soup. The strumming of emotion against lack of understanding, if you like. Non-communication of the highest form. Of course, it should have been read with a lot of Pinteresque silences, really to get it across, but I don't pretend to be an actor.' He began to undo the buttons of his shirt. 'What do you think? Do you think it'll give them an idea of the sort of thing I have in mind?'

'Oh yes,' I said. 'It'll do that very well.' A mean pause

in which he looked uncomfortable. So I went on: 'But it's difficult to be much of a judge not knowing anything about the characters. What happened in Scene One?'

He stood up, startled.

'Scene One? I haven't thought about that yet. This was just – a fragment, a particle of the play I thought worth getting down on to paper while the words leaped through my head.' He threw his shirt on the floor and undid the belt, and flies of his shorts. 'Hell, it's far too hot to go on working. We'll take a cottage on Lake Como in the autumn, perhaps. I could work very well, there, in the cool.' His shorts dropped to the floor and he stretched his arms high about his head. 'Let's sleep for a couple of hours, then go for a swim, then go out to dinner at that place you like along the coast, and dance. Would you like that?'

'Lovely.'

He padded towards the bed.

'You've still got your hat on,' I said. He threw that, too, onto the floor and lay beside me.

He lay beside me, naked, on top of the bedclothes, holding my hand.

'You're beautiful, Suki Soo,' he said, with his eyes shut. 'There's never been a luckier man.'

'Nonsense.'

'It's true. Beautiful, brown, warm, gay, loving. What more could a man want?' He hoisted himself up on one elbow and looked down at me. Arms, legs and face an incongruous red against the flat whiteness of the rest of him. 'I feel so loving towards you I don't know what to do with myself. How can I ever tell you how much I love you?' He flung himself on top of me, his hands parting my bathing robe, his tongue swooping into my mouth. His body was hot and heavy. He was hard against my thigh, breathing fast, shuddering.

'What's the matter?' He rolled off me again. 'Do I smell of garlic, or something?'

'Not much,' I said.

'Don't you want me?' I didn't answer. 'Don't you like it in the afternoon? Is it too soon after lunch? We'll wait a while.' He lay back on his pillow but still held my hand.

'I think I'm nearly asleep,' I said. We lay in silence for a while, looking at the ceiling. Then:

'Don't you ever feel anything violent?' he asked.

'How do you mean?'

'Well, I think it could be said I *express* my love for you. I want you all the time, and show it, wouldn't you say?'

'Yes.'

'But you have a funny way of expressing your love for me. You don't do anything. In fact, you crudely resist me sometimes.' He watched one of his feet as he bent each toe slowly in turn, as if he played a five-toe exercise. 'I mean, sometimes, when we're walking down a street or going to a theatre together, say, and I want to take your arm or hold your hand, you don't do anything or say anything, but you just make it very clear you don't want me to touch you. Don't you?'

'I admit I'm not by nature demonstrative. But then you're very calculated.'

'Nonsense, darling. What utter nonsense you talk. If there was ever a spontaneous lover, it's me. Think of the mornings – working mornings at that – we've had breakfast and I've said: "Let's go back to bed." '

'They've hardly been spontaneous,' I said.

'You silly old Suki Soo,' he said, rolling over towards

me, 'you've got on that funny hard voice that means you're a thousand miles away from me. Come on, cheer up. Smile. We're on holiday, remember? We're having a lovely time.'

I smiled. Encouraged, he let two fingers walk up to my breast like a child pretending to be a spider.

'I love you,' he said. 'Do you know how much I love you? I love you, I love you, I love you.' The fingers walked over to the other breast. 'Do you love me?'

'Yes.'

'How much?'

'I don't know. How can I measure?'

'Do you need me?'

'I expect so.'

'Do you want me?'

'I expect so.'

Sudden heat, a blackness in the shade of his heavy face. His tongue, enormous in my mouth, loiters at the roots of one tooth, then shambles on to another. Three more days till the aeroplane home. Sing things, sing things. *Te voglio bene tanto tanto, bene tanto tanto....* how did it go then? Count things. How many people at the table next to us at lunch? Three. Remember things. The fat woman wore a red dress. Very good. And the others? Now my nose squashed flat under his, spreading across my face, setting like fungi. His hand, confoundedly gentle and nosy, prying over my stomach, and up and down and up and down –

'Jonathan! Stop it! Stop it!' He rolls off me, a freak tide ebbing in fright.

'What on earth's the matter? What have I done now?'

I stand, pulling at the belt of the bathing robe. The floor tiles warm from the sun under my feet. I look at him, quickly crumpling, hurt.

'You must have overdone the sun,' he says at once, covering his anger. 'I told you you would.'

I sit on the bed again, thankful.

'That must be it, I'm sorry.' Silence. To calm, or to attack? I wonder which he will choose.

'Go to sleep, darling. You'll feel better when you wake up. As I said, the sun, and all that lunch. . . .' His voice full of care. I sleep.

When I woke up, some hours later, he had opened the shutters. A dusky mauve sky, a strip of mercury sea through the balcony railings. On the table a bottle of champagne stood in a primitive bucket of ice. I could hear Jonathan moving about in the bathroom. He came in, tying a blue-flowered tie that matched his blue flowered shirt and blue Terylene trousers. He indicated the champagne.

'Non-vintage, I'm afraid, but it's the best they could do. I thought it'd be nice to wake up to.'

'Lovely. Thank you.'

'At least it's cold.' He fingered the bottle, opened it easily and filled the glasses. 'After this you must have a slow bath, and put on those beautiful lilac trousers, and then we'll take one of those awful tourist carriage that you're always on about and go to the *Prima Trattoria*. I've booked a table.'

I tried the champagne. It was warm and sweet. Jonathan knew I had never liked it, but this was no reason to stop him ordering it for special occasions.

'Do you really need to book a table at the one restaurant in a small village two miles from anywhere?'

'I suppose not. But I like booking tables, don't I? You must let me book my tables in peace.' He smiled. 'Anyway. It's booked. Feeling better?'

'I'm fine.'

'It was only the sun – '

' – and all that lunch.'

'And all that lunch, yes, as I said.'

'Yes, yes.'

Jonathan refilled his glass and took my hand.

'You're not cross with me, darling?'

'No, why should I be?'

'I just thought you might be.' He cleared his throat. 'I was thinking, while you were asleep. I was thinking, we mustn't let this sort of thing get us down.'

'What sort of thing?'

'The sort of thing that happened this afternoon. It's not important.'

'What isn't important?'

'Well, we mustn't make a fuss about it, worry ourselves about it. The thing is, my love, in the long run sex doesn't matter. You know that, I know that.' I sat up and he gave me his arm to help me off the low bed. He smelt of lemoney after-shave. 'Well, when I say that, you know what I mean. I simply mean it shouldn't become too important, should it? There are lots of other things besides, aren't there, that are so much more important? And anyway, everyone has their off moments, don't they? – '

'I'm going for my bath,' I said. 'I absolutely agree.' He followed me into the bathroom and turned on the taps.

'So we won't make a fuss, we'll forget all about it,' he said, 'and I'm sorry if I was – a bore.'

'Of course you weren't,' I said. 'I don't know what came over me. I'm sorry too.'

He sat on the edge of the bath while I washed, playing

with a sponge. Filling it with water and squeezing it, filling it with water and squeezing it.

'So what we'll do is, we'll have a lovely dinner and lots of drink, and dance a bit, and talk to that nice man at the bar. Then we'll come back here, and it'll be nice and cool. And then, if you can bear it, if you're feeling like it, that is, we'll try again.'

As David Roberts said, Jonathan was indeed a loving man.

*

'Funny,' said Mrs Fox, 'this is the very bench we met on.'

It was eleven o'clock in the morning of a mild January day. Mrs Fox and I had been walking through the park feeding the birds. We were going to have lunch in a cottage restaurant she knew in Kensington where they sold home-made pies and cakes. But it was too early yet, and warm enough to sit.

'Oh yes,' she went on, 'I shan't be likely to forget that day. Edith's last outing, that was. And you all in black, looking very down. But then you'd been to that funeral, hadn't you? One of your husbands. – It doesn't seem like five months ago all that happened, Edith dying, does it? – Lovely yellow, that.' She pointed towards some early yellow crocuses nearby. 'Yellow was Henry's favourite colour. We always had yellow crocuses, just like those, in a bowl in the front room, every spring. But of course what Henry really liked was daffodils. You've never seen a man like him for daffodils. They were the first flowers he ever gave me. Bunches and bunches of them. He must have bought up a whole flower stall, I think, honestly, and he was only a student at the time – what it must of cost him. As a matter of a fact I wanted daffodils, for that very

reason, for his coffin. But it was the wrong time of year. I
went to all the flower shops I knew for miles, and I said
I must have daffodils. Forced, I said, if need be, as long
as they were daffodils. Oh madam, there are limits to
forcing, they told me. They said I couldn't have any, no
matter what I paid. I don't think they cared, really. Not
by the way they spoke to me. Forced daffodils! I might
have been asking for an extinct plant, the reception they
gave me.'

She took a handful of crumbs from a small paper bag
and threw them to some starlings.

'I forgot to tell you,' she said, 'I've got two tickets for a
pop concert at the Albert Hall to-morrow night. I was
wondering if you would like to come? I'm not sure of the
name of the group, but it's their farewell concert, I heard
people saying in the queue. They're bound to have lots of
those amplifier things – they almost burst the Hall with
noise. I've heard that sort of thing there before. It should
be good.'

'That would be lovely,' I said. To-morrow night Joshua
was working very late, he said. Two starlings came right
up to Mrs Fox's feet.

'February,' she said. 'My, it's almost February. Your
decision's coming up then, isn't it?'

'Yes,' I said.

'What's it going to be?'

'I don't know.'

'Well, it's better to admit you don't know than to
pretend you do, as Henry always used to say. He was the
quickest doctor to admit he didn't know I ever met. More
like him would save patients a lot of time.' Her bag of
crumbs empty, she touched the Poppy Day poppy in her
hat.

'That reminds me,' she said, 'I never told you what they did that day.' She rubbed the rings on her bare hand and gave a small kick towards the starlings, as if their greedy pecking, now that the crumbs were finished, suddenly annoyed her. 'As soon as she died, that is. As soon as she died, before they'd even closed her eyes, they pulled the bedclothes back. Her nightgown had all wormed its way up round her, if you know what I mean, and her body, it was like a skeleton. Imagine it! There was never a more modest woman all her life, and yet the minute she dies they expose her. I pulled the sheets up again because her nightgown was all under her. I couldn't have moved that without moving her. But that bossy matron – trust her to nose her way in at the dramatic moment – was on to me in no time. "What do you think you're doing?" she says. "She'll be cold," I says. – Stupid, I know, but I felt she would be cold. The matron laughed at me. "Cold?" she says. "She'll be cold in a jiffy on this earth, no matter how many blankets, and if she's been a good woman she'll be warm in Heaven." I'll always remember how she said that. Then she told me to go away, unless I wanted to watch the preparations.

'The funny thing is, ever since then, and this is what's troubling me, I've never been able to think of Edith with her clothes on again. I lie awake for hours in the night, sometimes, trying to imagine her in her brown wool dress, or her navy floral summer one, or her best dress, the greeny crêpe. I knew them all well, all those dresses, but for the life of me I can't imagine them on her any more. What I do is, I lay a dress out on a chair in one corner of my mind, then she walks in from the other side, like in a film. She puts on the dress, slowly, like she used to dress, and stands with her back to me zipping it up. When she turns round again I can see her face, clear as anything, but the dress isn't there. She's naked. All I can see is her poor thin body, like it was the day she died. And I hadn't seen it bare for fifty years, remember. "Edith," I says to her in my mind, "get dressed Edith. You mustn't stand about like that or you'll get cold. . ." But she just looks at me, silent like she often was, silent and bare and getting cold. . . .'

Without warning it began to rain, gentle rain from the mild sky. Mrs Fox stood up. As she rose she gave a small gasp. I gave her my arm but she ignored it.

'For heaven's sake, child, I'm not having a heart attack, you know. It's just indigestion. I tried frozen hamburgers last night, all laid out with the rest of the meal in a tinfoil tray. All I had to do was warm them up. They must have done it. That's the trouble with instant food.' We began to walk towards Kensington.

'Lots of funny things, this morning, if you think about it,' she said. 'That other time, you remember? That other time it began to rain upon us too.'

*

Somewhere in a place full of light further lights explode. Way out beyond the petty rim of the globe there is a soaring and a swooping and an ultimate meeting as flesh dissolves flesh, bones are liquid, blood flames. On the way back there is a lesser light, a more ordinary light, shaped like a window. And the blare of inaudible music is scraped to nothing but the tick of an ordinary clock.

Joshua is kissing me, my eyes, my hair. He is slung all over me, his arms and legs heavy as fallen boughs.

'Funny Face?'

'Joshua?'

169

'I was only just awake, too.'

'I know.' I hold him. He is soft. He is warm.

'Funny Face?'

'Yes? What?'

'Nothing, really.' He falls to my side now, his head on my breast. 'You're very *small*.' My smile moves his hair.

'You're huge.'

'Like that?'

'Um.' I wriggle. 'You know what?' I say. 'It's Sunday.'

'Sunday?'

'Sunday.'

'Imagine. Sunday. I didn't know that.' He moves higher on the pillow now, so that he can look down at me.

'We can spend all day in bed.' I rub his scratchy chin. 'I've got kippers for very late breakfast.' He twists a strand of my hair in his fingers, pulling it quite hard.

'You funny old planner. You must have worked it all out yesterday.'

'So? Normally, you say I'm not efficient.'

'I wouldn't like you to be any efficienter. What did Jonathan think?'

'He made up for anything I lacked in efficiency. He stocked up the whole store cupboard, one week. Things I would never have thought about. Only the best brands of everything. He was a terrible snob about marmalade. Nothing but Elsenham.'

'You speak of him with great affection.'

'It was rather endearing, his brand-snobbism. That's all.'

Joshua reached for a cigarette. Our legs stayed in a confused knot.

'You realise it's the end of January?' he asked.

'Everybody's been reminding me,' I said.

'I have to leave for Mexico in three weeks. And you have to make your decision.' He smoked almost to the end of his cigarette in silence. 'Are you going back to Jonathan?'

I sighed.

'I don't *know*,' I said. 'There's time.'

'Not a lot.' He crushed the cigarette out on his thumb. 'And sadly, I'll have to miss the kippers, unless you'd keep them for to-night.'

'Why?'

'Work.'

'But it's Sunday.'

'So you say. I'm sorry, Face, really I am. But I've got to get this thing finished before we leave. When I say work, I mean work, you idiot. I'm not off with a blonde.'

'With Annabel.'

'I'm not off with Annabel.'

'I believe you, but you're always *going*.'

'Cheer up. I'm always having to cheer you up. I'll be back about five, I expect. You can have a whole day to think in.'

He sat up, so I sat up.

'I don't need a whole day,' I said. 'I've made up my mind. I'm not going back to Jonathan.'

Joshua smiled disbelievingly.

'How odd. If I'd had to put a bet on it, I would have sworn you would have decided the other way. So what will you do instead?'

'Stay with you, of course.'

'That might be difficult, fixing for you to come to Mexico. But you could wait for me to come back.'

We looked at each other for a long time.

'All right,' I said.

'I haven't been very nice to you, really, when you think about it. I can't think why you want to stay.'

'Don't you want me to?'

He laughed.

'Face, you must know me by now. As I never know what I want in the abstract, I'm usually fairly satisfied with whatever I have in reality.'

'That doesn't sound as if you would be exactly desperate without me.'

He took my chin in his hand and lifted my face towards him.

'You funny thing,' he said. 'You funny, small thing.'

Very soon after he left the flat forgetting, as he sometimes did, to say good-bye.

Chapter Twelve

The first time I discovered I was pregnant was in Portsmouth, ten days after Richard had sailed for Barcelona. I had felt sick for several mornings, and skipped those hushed breakfasts alone in the dining-room. Finally, I went to a doctor. 'Two months gone,' he said.

It was news for my next letter to Richard. '*Won't that be lovely?*' I wrote, '*I'll be having it in April.*' I sent the letter express. The baby would be a girl, I decided. Called Ophelia.

That night a searing pain strangled my stomach and I began to bleed. I rushed from the bathroom, a bath towel between my legs, and picked up the old, heavy telephone beside the bed. The receptionist, who had taken the job because it fitted in with her insomnia, took her usual three minutes to answer.

'What is it, dear? It's getting on for midnight.'

'I need a doctor.'

'A doctor?'

'Yes. Quickly, please.' The blood was beginning to soak the towel.

'Is there anything the matter?'

'*Yes*. I need a doctor.'

'Is there anything I can do? I took a course in nursing, once, you know, myself – .'

'Please,' I said. She seemed immune to the urgency in my voice. 'Please just get me a doctor.'

'Well, Dr Harris, I know he's on to-night. But then you

know he hasn't been well, himself, lately. I wouldn't like to call him out unless it was really urgent.'

'It is,' I screamed.

Dr Harris arrived an hour later. The receptionist let him into my room.

'Ooh dear,' she said, when she saw me, 'you did need a doctor.' Dr Harris sent her to ring for an ambulance and immeasurable time later I groaned and cursed on the stiff white sheets of a hospital bed. By the next morning it was all over.

My mother came down to Portsmouth to drive me back to the hotel. She had gold chains on her crocodile shoes to match the handles of her crocodile bag. She was dismayed by the fact that I had been treated the same as everyone else.

'Good heavens, darling, why on earth didn't they get you into a private room?' She wrapped a rug round me in the car and said I looked pale. 'You're such a *worry*, Clare. Are you sure you don't want to come home for a few days? You know you can come whenever you like.' I thanked her, but declined. She was used to my declining most of her invitations.

Back at the hotel she filled my hot water bottle and put a vast basket of fruit on the table beside my bed. It was wrapped in cellophane paper and topped with a cellophane bow.

'There are figs, somewhere,' she said, brightly, with the confidence that figs would cheer my day, 'I know you've always loved figs.'

She paced about my room uncertain what to do, picking up then putting down her precious handbag. We listened to the rattle of the central heating and the croak of gulls, clear against the traffic noise, outside the window.

Finally she picked up a photograph of Richard from the dressing-table, stiff and alert in his uniform.

'What a good looking man Richard is, darling, isn't he? So mature, I've always thought. Do you suppose he'll fly back?'

'Not for a moment,' I said. 'Anyhow, there's no point.'

'I suppose not.' She picked up her bag again. 'I must be off, I suppose. Are you sure there's nothing else you want? Just let me know if there is. Ring me any time, won't you?' She bent down to kiss me. She smelt sickeningly of the oily gardenia scent she always wore. 'I hope you don't mind my going, but you know what it is. It's such a busy time of year, one way and another. – No, no. It hasn't *been* a trouble, coming all the way down here. You mustn't think that.'

Three days later came the reply to my first letter to Richard. *'How lovely, little one, as you say. I'm sure it'll be a boy. We can call it either Richard or Clive – both family names. You choose. I don't mind as long as it's one of those. I will, of course, expect him to follow in the naval tradition of our family. Anything else would be unthinkable. Take care of yourself and I'll be home long before April. . .'*

That night he rang me from Barcelona.

'So sorry to hear, little one.' He sounded quite sad. 'Still, these things happen. Don't take it too badly. We'll try again next time I'm back.'

'Of course,' I said. I felt no enthusiasm about starting again. My stomach ached and my room was a huge, vacant gap all around me. 'I wish,' I said, 'I could join you in Spain. I'd like to be with you.' There was a long pause.

'Little one,' he said, at last. 'I don't think you should. For your own sake. You'd do much better to recover where

175

you are, quietly. I'm out most of the day, and you know
what the food's like over here.'

'None of that would matter,' I said.

'I don't think you should,' he repeated. I felt cold. My
hand began to sweat on the receiver of the telephone.

'I could spend most of my time lying on the beach,' I
said.

'The beach isn't very nice.'

'Well, I could drive about.'

'You don't speak Spanish.'

'I could get by.'

'I don't think you should.' He sighed. I sighed.

'All right,' I said. 'I'll stay here.'

'Oh, little one.' His relief was infinite. 'I think you'll
find I'm right. I'll call you again soon. Or you ring me,
any time, if you want anything, won't you?'

I got up the next day and went back to normal life. The
days went slowly as they had done before. Richard didn't
ring again. Three weeks went by. Then a letter:

'*Little one,*

*How can I ever explain? You know I once told you about a
woman called Matilda? Well, in a word, I love her. I have
fought it, she has fought it, but there is no denying it. We are in
love with one another. We live together and want to get married
one day. None of that is to say I don't love you. In a strange way
I still do, and perhaps always will. I will always think of you as
my Little One. Please, please don't take it too badly. These things
happen. Perhaps we should never have married. Your mother
always said I was baby snatching. But still, I believed in it, in us,
at the time. Oh dear, I never have been very good at letters. I'm
putting it all very badly. You can cite Matilda, of course. Your
father will know a good solicitor. I think of you often. I wish this*

needn't have happened just after the miscarriage, but love attaches little importance to timing, does it, and I felt it would be wrong to keep it from you any longer.

Please forgive me if you can, and don't think badly of the many good times we've had together.

Love, Richard.'

*

The second time, with only two weeks to go before Joshua went to Mexico, I felt sick in the evenings. I had kept it from him for a couple of weeks, but decided to tell him when he came home that Sunday from work.

'Two bits of news in one day,' I said. 'Not only am I not going back to Jonathan – '

' – but you're pregant too, I suppose.' He was flipping his vodka backwards and forwards in the glass.

'Exactly. How did you know?'

'You look pregnant,' he said. 'You've looked very – careful for the last two weeks.' I laughed.

'Aren't you pleased?'

'Of course I am.' He paused. 'Did you mean to?'

'No, honestly.'

'I believe you.' He smiled, quite kindly. 'The only thing is, don't forget, I haven't said anything about marriage.'

'Nor have I,' I said.

'So what are you going to do about it?'

'Do about it?'

'Are you going to *have* it?'

'*Have* it? – '

'Are you going to have it, I said?'

I paused to think, pushing the ice cubes round my glass with a numb finger. At last I said:

'Of course I'm going to have it.'

'I see.' He got up and went over to the table for a packet of cigarettes, not looking at me. 'If you changed your mind, I know a particularly good doctor, even though it's all legal now.'

'But I'm not going to change my mind. Don't you see? I *want* it.' Joshua sighed and went back to another seat, farther from me.

'In that case,' he said, 'you'd better find us somewhere to live. Quickly. We couldn't stay here with a child.'

'Of course not.' Potential houses. Prams. Joshua lifting it up to look at it when he came home. Warm milk, small fingers. I began to drown in a heavy calm. Mrs Fox would knit things. 'And there's just one other thing,' I said.

'I know what that is, too.' Joshua shifted about on the sofa, unusually restless. 'As you're pregnant, it would be quicker and easier and generally more convenient if Jonathan cited me in the divorce. Yes, I accept that too. Is there anything else, while we're about it?' He was frowning. I got up and went over to him.

'What's the matter?' I asked.

'Go and sit down or you'll feel sick.' I stood my ground. 'Go on. You must take care.' He seemed briefly concerned. I went back to the sofa.

'About the divorce – ' I said.

'There's no more to be said.' He stubbed his cigarette out with his thumb. 'I've agreed happily to being cited. You go ahead and do whatever it is you have to do, as fast as possible, for the sake of the baby. I won't make any kind of fuss, I promise, and the whole pattern will fall into place. We will all play our parts, Jonathan and I, I've no doubt, just as you imagined. It will all be very neat and easy and tidy. No fuss. First husband dies, second husband is divorced, lover agrees to support both you and his child. What more could you want? – Oh, and probably, if you play your cards right, which no doubt being you you will, one day I might even offer you marriage as well. So there's a lovely future for you, all planned out. All lovely – '

' – Joshua!' I rose in a daze of nausea and tears.

'Sit *down*. You'll feel sick. Stop stomping about.'

'I *do* feel sick.'

'Sit down, then.' I sat. There was a long silence. Neither of us could think of anything to say. Then:

'I won't have it if you really don't want it,' I said. 'I could have an abortion.'

'No, no. You wouldn't want that.'

'Would you?'

'Probably not, when it came to it. I'm sorry, Face. As usual, I went too far.' He smiled. 'But you've sprung a lot on me in one day.' I smiled back.

'Oughtn't we do something?' I asked.

'You have an infallibly awful sense of occasion,' he said, 'but as there's no food in the place, I suppose we ought. If you're not feeling too sick, we'd better go out to dinner.'

*

The morning Jonathan brought home the pink toy bear for our unconceived baby he also brought pink roses and the inevitable bottle of champagne.

'This is nothing,' he said, 'nothing compared with what I shall bring when the real time comes. You won't believe it. I shall have bells rung, guns fired, jewellery delivered. . . . You wait.' He was in one of his gayest moods, happy to be away from his study and the blank sheet of paper.

He scooped my hair up behind my ears and held it high in an untidy bun. 'My darling Suki Soo, if you could ever for one moment believe how much I loved you – ', he stooped to kiss the neck he had made naked, ' – well, you couldn't ever believe it. Now. Let's open the bottle.'

Jonathan toasted our future child. We sat there, side by side on the chintz sofa, hand in hand – his hands were always warm and very soft – Jonathan cooing about what he and his son would do together when the time came. He kissed me on the cheeks, the eyelids, the temples, his lips wet and bubbly with the champagne. He had taken off his coat. He sat in his braces, his shirt very white in the morning sun which slanted through the room and lit up the pot plants in their vases, still tied up in bows.

I drank till I felt weak and dizzy. I laughed and giggled and kissed Jonathan back, on the nose, on the puffy jaws that tasted of after-shave, and at last I was able to say, with all conviction, that I agreed with him. It would be nice to have his baby.

*

Joshua woke in the middle of the night. He put his hand on my stomach.

'The awful thing is, Face,' he said, 'that it looks as if I will probably have to be in Mexico for at least three months. Will you be all right?'

*

Some nights later I was wakened by sharp, familiar pains in my back and stomach. It was three o'clock. I woke Joshua.

'There's something wrong.'

'Oh God.' He put on the light. 'Same as before?' I

nodded. He smoothed his hand gently over my stomach and down between my legs. Then he drew it back to the light. It was covered in blood.

'So the plans have gone wrong after all,' I said.

'Shut up,' he said. 'Maybe we can save it.'

Everything happened very quickly. I heard him telephoning people, making arrangements in short snappy sentences. I heard my own moans as he lifted me from the bed, wrapped me in a blanket and carried me to the car. The leather of the car seat was very cold. As the engine shuddered to a start I bent double, trying to shut out the pain.

'Hold on, Face,' I think Joshua said. 'The doctor said it would be better if we got you in. I thought I could make it quicker than an ambulance.'

The car screamed through empty streets, the blood rushed warm down my legs.

'The floor of your car,' I kept saying. 'I'm sorry about the floor of your car.'

Someone met us with a stretcher. Grey corridors blistered with neon lights waved like streamers past my eyes. Then there was a white room that smelt of disinfectant. Badly drawn dog-roses on the beige curtains. A nurse bent over me. Three blackheads shaped like a clover leaf were stamped on the side of her nose, sharp points in her starchy skin. She gave me something bitter to drink. A doctor came in and patted me on the flanks like a friendly farmer.

'How is she feeling, then?' he asked Joshua, as if I wasn't there. He flicked down the sheets, lifted my nightgown and pulled the reading lamp, on its metal arm, towards him. Joshua held my hand.

Hours later the doctor came back again. His face was

stripped into a thousand coiling pieces as if it had been through a mincer.

'Good heavens, what a thing, you're biting the sheet, sheet, sheet, sheet. . . .' he said, his voice echoing away. I felt Joshua fold up both my hands like a ball of wool and hold them in both his. Then the doctor's voice came again.

'I'm afraid that's that,' he said. 'That's that, that's that, that's that. . .' I could hear watery noises on the lino floor, someone with a mop, the crackling of paper, nurses' quick feet going tap-tap, tap-tap, the dry rub of the doctor's hands. But when I opened my eyes they had all gone. All but Joshua.

'Oh, Face,' he said. 'Are you awake?' He bent his head down over mine. 'I didn't want that to happen, either.' Then he got up brusquely and strode over to another part of the room, so that without moving my head I couldn't see him any more.

'I'll leave you to sleep,' he said. 'I must go. It's getting on for eleven. The doctor said it would be a good idea for you to stay here for a few days. You're a bit torn about.' He returned to my bed and stood looking down at me.

'You must go,' I said, 'you'll be late.'

'Poor old Face,' he said.

*

Mrs Fox, of course, was my first visitor. She arrived with daffodils and a honeycomb later that afternoon.

'There was a helicopter going over towards Battersea Bridge,' she said. 'I saw it from the bus so I got out at the next stop and watched it go by. That's what made me late. The noise! Then there wasn't another bus for twenty minutes.' She dumped her parcels at the end of my bed and drew up an upright chair. This morning she had two poppies in her hat and the silver painted goose feathers, left over from Christmas Day, pinned to the lapel of her coat. She looked me up and down and pulled her chair nearer.

'Shall I tell you something? Last night I went to this Bach Society evening. Well, it was very interesting. We all sang for a couple of hours, then we went into the Meeting Room for coffee and sandwiches. The members, that is. It was a 'members only' night. The cream of the Bach followers they think they are, too. I wouldn't have joined them if I'd known what snobs they were.

'Anyhow. Roger Nevern, the young American conductor, you know, had agreed to come and meet us. He was half an hour late, which got some of them very worried. The coffee was finished. And when he did come, my! You could hear the gasps going up. All because his hair was long and he was wearing a lovely flowered shirt and tie. I suppose they expected white tie and tails. They could hardly sustain their titters, I can tell you. The rudeness of it, and he was being so polite, taking an interest in each one of us and repeating our names when he was introduced. When he'd gone they all huddled together, these old things, and the rumour was he'd been seen at another do in a pale blue fur coat almost down to his ankles. What a crime! I said. I felt I had to speak out. What a crime! I said, a blue fur coat. Well, they must have heard the note of sarcasm in my voice, because they all turned on me, you know, all their heads spun round simultaneously and they began to go at *me*, as if I was wearing blue fur.

'Well, they got as good as they gave, I can tell you. I told them what a bunch of hypocrites they were. Stupid old fools. If Shakespeare himself came back from the dead they'd expect him to be dressed by Moss Bros. Poor dears, they have no notion of genius. They are so confined by their own mistaken little priorities.' She smiled to herself and began to wander round the room. 'This is a nice place you're in,' she said, 'will you be out soon?'

'In a few days,' I said.

'When you're out we will all go to Brighton for some sea air. You need a bit of sea air. We'll go for the day. I'll ask Joshua to take us. We'll go and look for the house Edith and I were brought up in. I hear it's a bed and breakfast place now, but never mind. You need the sea air.'

When she had gone a young nurse with red hair came in with pills.

'What a night,' she said, brightly, 'we had the same thing happen next door. A very young couple. They'd only been married three months, too. We had a terrible time with the husband. I think he was rather the hysterical type, mind, but we had to give him sedatives. Your husband gone? Back to work, I suppose.'

It was easier not even to pause.

'Yes. He's very busy.'

'He'll be back,' she said, 'and you'll feel quite different in a few days, I can tell you.'

That afternoon was one of those slow, white afternoons that often happen in late winter, when shadowless light from the sky stretches taut across a window, flatter than the light of spring and more melancholy. On the table that made a bridge over the foot of my bed twelve daffodils, cruelly yellow against the white walls, squashed rigidly together in a tall, thin hospital vase. A thermometer stood in a glass of pink liquid, above the basin, and in a room so drained of colour the yellow of the flowers and the pink of the liquid jarred my eyes. My stomach ached. It was a scooped out hole. I could feel the shape of the hollow among my guts. I waited for it to wither, to close back into place, and the beat of the ache throbbed in my head like a chant.

The bed was uncomforting, narrow and hard. I stretched my feet down and felt the hardness of the iron bed-end. I turned away from the glare of light in the window, and shut my eyes.

*

I kept my eyes shut for several moments after the matron brusqued in on Sunday mornings, shouting at us with a vicious gaiety to get out of bed *quickly*, or else. She would clatter down the linoleum aisle between the two rows of beds, tweak back the thin curtains with a petulant snap, and stand triumphant as the daylight gushed in on us. I opened my eyes to watch her return journey. Barely raised the lids, for fear of catching her glance and having no energy to reject it. Through a blur of lashes I saw the familiar, low-slung calves that bulged just a few inches above the well-polished heels of her flat brown sensible walking shoes. A confident walk. Miss Peel was full of confidence and authority. She had an amazing head for name-tapes, too. She could recall the precise condition of scores of pairs of bras, vests and knickers, and whether or not they were adequately marked. Her anecdotes, which invariably appealed to her rather more than they did to her audience, were all about underwear. There was one old girl, famous in Miss Peel's memory, who went through four pairs of gym knickers in one term. In her own mind, Miss Peel felt her sense of humour to be a little *risqué*, and among the juniors she managed to curb her conversation to shoes, socks and overwear; but her heart was not in it.

Her usual Sunday call echoed down the dormitory.

'Nylons for those going out with parents, lisle for everybody else, of course, and no powder for *any* noses, or there'll be trouble.'

Sunday at school was an icy, lumbering day that bore no relation to the rest of the week. A gap to be endured until the bustle and normality of Monday: a day when the passing of time was unusually slow and the strictures of confinement almost intolerable. We were forced to observe the Lord's day of rest with stalwart exactitude, and smarten ourselves up to a standard that would delight Christ Himself should He care suddenly to descend. Scratchy overcoats. Straight seamed, lumpy stockings thick as gloves; pathetically drab brown dresses which, in an attempt to liven up, we scrunched in at the waists with huge elastic belts – the most desirable accessories of the early fifties.

On Sundays we wrote uncomplaining letters to our parents and walked in crocodile to church. We were allowed to listen to classical music and read good books, and there were hundreds-and-thousands on whatever the pudding at lunch. But it was the evenings, the fragile evenings full of the sad thundering church bells from the priory church, that filled us with the wild folly of anticipation and the tremulous ache of longing to be free. We would sit on the summer lawn, rugs spread over pine needles from the vast trees, eyes cast down over our pieces of sewing. The headmistress with her tired Rosetti face, curved eyebrows and wispy hair was the only one to sit on a chair. A bible lay on her lap. She would glance, as she glanced a thousand times a day, up to the hills; two dramatic great purple swellings in the sky now, nothing like the scurvy lumps they were to walk over, diseased with sweet-papers and council notices. The headmistress believed in her range of hills. She took strength from them. 'I will lift up mine eyes,' as she so often said.

On Sunday evenings she would talk to her seniors about going out into the world, as the time approached – the great unprotective world beyond the school gate. Her voice was always full of promise.

'Always remember, girls, to kick against the pricks, as St Paul said.' All would be fine if we kicked against them. She lulled us in to security. 'And remember, too, that if God be for you, who can be against you?' She spoke often of the love of God, never of the love of man. We wondered if she had ever been loved herself, by man as well as God. She was so confident of the happy outcome of loving God. She looked happy on it. And the school magazine was full of the news of old girls who, having learnt like us to love Him, had on the way found husbands too, and were leading lives of pleasurable security, as the child-bearing wives of Midland farmers, solicitors, humble aristocrats and industrial tycoons.

On those Sunday evenings on the shadowy rugs, there wasn't one of us who didn't believe that it would all fall into place for us, too. We felt a blinding, overpowering resolve to make our own future work; to kick against the pricks, to stick to what we promised, to go on believing. Trembling with good intention, tears scalded our eyes.

So we left school with all the privilege of having been warned. We left believing in God, in Wordsworth, in our role in life as good wives and mothers. For several years,

187

in fact, some of us still remembered, from time to time, how these old beliefs felt.

*

'Soo,' said Jonathan, once, 'however much I fail you, will you go on forgiving me?' We were having breakfast in a hard, high and narrow bed somewhere, and he had egg on his chin.

*

Joshua came back in the evening.

'Feeling better?' he asked. I raised myself on the pillows and he kissed my forehead. He looked round the bare room. 'There were such awful flowers on the barrow downstairs that I knew you'd know they had come from there, so I didn't get any. I'm sorry.'

'That's all right.' The hole in my stomach felt smaller. Joshua grinned.

'You don't look your best, Face.'

'I don't feel my best.'

'But well enough to come home to-morrow? It'd be nice to have you there for the last few days. I leave on Monday. It's all finally fixed.' To-day was Thursday.

'Of course I'll come,' I said.

'Good.' He sat on the chair close to my bed and took my hand. His heel began to tap on the floor. 'Face, Face,' he said quietly.

'What is it?'

'I don't know. All this muddle. There doesn't seem much point now, does there?'

'Not much point in what?'

'You know. In going ahead. Breaking up your marriage. Living together.' For a moment or two I thought of moving my hand from under his. But I had no energy to make the gesture.

'Oh,' I said. 'I see what you've been thinking.'

'If we'd had the baby, then of course – '

' – of course it would have been different.'

'Of course.' Silence. Then I said:

'What a pity I'm not better at having children. I didn't realise, when the miscarriage began, two things were at stake.'

Joshua thumped the bed and stopped tapping his heel at last.

'For God's sake don't say things like that. You make me sound more of a shit then even I thought I was.'

'Sorry.'

He bent very near to me, holding up his hands expressively, like a man trying to sell something.

'Listen, Face. Listen to me. You've got to go back to Jonathan. You've known that, I've known that, really, all along. You can't leave someone, just like that, just because your heart doesn't leap about any more every time he comes into the room, and he annoys you the way he eats his kippers. That's not what marriage is about, if it's worth anything at all. Besides, you've told me hundreds of times you love him, in a way, haven't you? Perhaps that way is good enough. And hundreds of times you've missed him, I know. Even though you haven't said anything. But I know, because I've watched you. Sometimes, when I've been particularly cruel or thoughtless, I've seen your face. I know what you've thought. You've thought: maybe Jonathan isn't particularly clever or witty or interesting, but at least he's kind, and he's always loving and reasonable. You've thought that, haven't you? Am I wrong?'

'Go on,' I said.

'My trouble,' he said, 'my trouble is that I'm not *present* in all that I do. Baldwin once pointed out that one should be present in order to be sensual. I'm cruel because I'm thoughtless, and I'm thoughtless about one thing because I'm thinking about another, and so often I get my priorities wrong. And when it comes to you – I have thought about it so much, honestly I have – I don't think I'm prepared to give up enough for you. I'm too unreliable, too unwittingly unkind. I would only make you unhappy. Perhaps I don't care enough – and there you are, you see, that's cruel.' He began to play with my fingers, hot stony fingers at the end of a weightless arm. Then he smiled at me, quite cheerfully. 'At least you could rely on Jonathan's constant loving. It's a great virtue, consistency. Besides, think how he must miss you, how much he must want you back. Anybody who had been loved by you, and has lost you, would want you back.'

I shut my eyes. Images shifted as in a gently shaken kaleidoscope. The flaring colours of butterflies, a great arc of Norfolk sky, the spray of sand in windy dunes, omelettes on Formica tables, the shimmer of blue sequins.

'How do you know we'd survive, Face?' Joshua was saying. 'Please open your eyes.'

I did. His pale face, now so near, was a fall of imperfect skin – pitted, lined, shadowy. His dark eyes were far back out of reach, sealed behind reflecting lenses.

'Perhaps we wouldn't,' I said.

He sat back. A confusion of expressions crossed his face – surprise, relief, disappointment, perhaps.

'So what will you do?' he asked.

'Go back,' I said, 'of course.'

After a long time of silence he fell upon me, kissing me, touching my hair, my ears, my breasts.

'You're right, you're right, you're right,' he kept saying. 'We're both right, aren't we? But oh Christ, Face.' He sat up again, still holding both my hands. 'It'll be funny, after six months.'

'It's been a pretty good time,' I said. I heard myself laughing, a sort of small, quiet snort. 'Joshua Heron', I said.

'Mrs Lyall?'

'Joshua Heron, now it's all over, now everything is over, I feel terribly, terribly tired.' He smiled back.

'Don't go to sleep just yet. I've got something for you.' He felt in his pocket. 'I didn't know what to get, really, so I went to Mrs Fox for advice. I'm no good at presents.'

I opened a small box. On a bed of cotton-wool lay her star-sapphire ring, the colour of milky forget-me-nots. When I moved it, even in the fading evening light, the spikes of a star, dazzling razor lines, split the stone.

'She gave it to me,' Joshua was saying. 'She said I could do what I liked with it. What else could I do?'

At that moment, I think it was, when he put it on my finger and held my hand up to the light, I began to cry. Weakly, hopelessly.

'Shut up,' he said. 'Shut up or I'll think you don't like it. It looks marvellous. Much better than on her old hands.'

'I'm thinking of how she'll miss it. She must have been rubbing it with her other hand for years.' I was also wondering what Joshua would do that evening. I didn't want him to be unfaithful now, not before Monday, when our term officially ended. It was a wasted evening, being in bed.

'I know what you're thinking,' he said. 'But you needn't worry. I'm taking Mrs Fox to the Festival Hall. Verdi.'

I stopped crying. Calm, calm, calm.

'But you hate that sort of music,' I said.

'It'll be different with Mrs Fox. She'll explain it all to me.'

'I wish I was coming too.'

'You don't like Verdi either.'

'No.'

'I wish you were, though. But still, we'll go to Brighton on Sunday, by special request of Mrs Fox. Would you like that?'

'Oh yes. I'd like that.'

'We'll do that, then.' He paused, bent down, took my face in his hands and kissed my eyes, forcing them to shut.

'It's very odd,' I said, half-asleep, 'how the most difficult decisions to make are the easiest ones to change.'

'I daresay,' said Joshua, 'I'll think of you. I daresay I'll think of you all through the Verdi.'

Chapter Thirteen

Almost as soon as I arrived back at the flat David Roberts
rang.

'Your friendly adviser here again,' he said. 'Your time
is up, old thing.'

'I know, I know.'

'If it will fit in with your plans, Jonathan would like to
meet you at six o'clock on Tuesday evening.'

'Why then, particularly?'

'Because that is exactly and precisely when the six
months will be up.' He coughed. 'As a matter of fact,
though don't say you know this, Jonathan is already back
in London. I saw him last night. He looked very fit.
Remarkably well, considering.'

'Good.'

'Might I be so bold as to ask what is going to happen?
I mean, after all, I'm the one who's been keeping the two
of you in touch, as it were.' He laughed to himself.

'I'm sorry,' I said, 'but I can't very well tell you before
I tell Jonathan. Ring on Tuesday evening.'

'Ah well, I won't press you. Anyhow, you know me –
the eternal optimist. I'll be thinking of you both.'

'Thank you.'

'Shall I tell him that will be all right, then? Six o'clock,
Tuesday?'

'Yes please. Tell him I'll be there. And thank you for all
your trouble.'

'That's all right, old thing. Any time.'

*

Sunday we went to Brighton, the three of us. Mrs Fox wore an old musquash coat dyed blue. The dyeing had not been wholly successful. Streaks of dull brown rippled through the dull blue.

'I was reading about those fun furs,' she explained. 'That's what gave me the idea.' On her hat an Alexandra Rose Day rose and a Poppy Day poppy were intertwined with a shining cherry I had not seen before. She rubbed uneasily at the finger on which she used to wear the star-sapphire ring. Now it was replaced by a dim moonstone, whose feel was still strange to her.

It was a cold, bright day. We parked the car in one of the crescents and walked to a small restaurant for lunch. Inside, the dark patterned carpets felt peculiarly soft after the sting of the pavements, and our breath jerked into the air in silver globes.

We climbed a winding staircase to an upstairs room. It was half-filled with people who talked in quiet Sunday voices. On the unoccupied tables stiff white napkins stood on empty plates like solitary flames, and a shaft of winter sun lit up a trolley of puddings. We chose a corner table with comfortable bench seats. Mrs Fox and I sat together with Joshua opposite. He chose things for us from the long menu. The last lunch this, perhaps, with Joshua, for ever. And yet, no feeling of frustration, no warning of sentimental tears. Instead, a surprising sensation of peace, like the unique luxury of stretching between sleep and wakefulness.

Mrs Fox took off her coat. Her long strings of bead necklaces clacked against her plate as she leant over it. As she chattered I only half-listened to her, leaving Joshua to reply. I studied him with intense concentration, trying to imprint every small movement on my mind. The way he cut his roll – he cut the top off like other people slice the top off a boiled egg, then, without looking, pulled out the doughy inside with finger and thumb, rolling the bits into hard pellets and dropping them under the table-cloth. The way he looked right into his glass when he took a sip of wine: the way he caught his bottom lip under his top teeth to trap a smile while he listened to Mrs Fox. And when the story came to an end, the way he laughed with his mouth wide open, so that the polo-neck of his jersey was tipped over by his chin. I pushed the plate of butter towards him and briefly he held my hand.

'You're beautiful to-day, Face,' he said. Quietly, so that Mrs Fox shouldn't hear.

When lunch was over we walked along the front. Joshua between Mrs Fox and me. We each took an arm.

'In the old days,' Mrs Fox was saying, 'the bands in the tea-houses along the front were something remarkable. During the season, Edith and I spent most of our afternoons drinking tea in one or other of the places, just listening. There was one place we especially liked, I remember. Rusco's, I think it was called. They did a very good chocolate cake. It was so full of rum you had to eat it with a spoon. Well, at Rusco's, the leader of the band took a fancy to Edith. I could tell. He would always give a special bow in her direction at the end of every piece. He always wore a carnation in his buttonhole, this man, and he had the shiniest black hair I ever saw, right flat on his head, almost like another skin. – Edith was pretty in those days, mind. She had curls all round her face. Well, one day the waiter brought us over a little note from the bandleader. *Ladies*, it said, *is there any request you would like us to play for you?* But Edith, being so shy, just turned her head away and blushed. After that, she wouldn't go to Rusco's any more. I often think of the chance she might have missed.'

It was quite warm, walking fast, in the sun, although a sharp wind was blowing from the sea. The grey waves dipped and swooped restlessly, and above them a few gulls imitated their movements in the air.

'It's funny about Brighton,' said Mrs Fox, 'it's where all the best things have happened to me. It was on the train from Victoria to Brighton that I met Henry. In truth, I was going to Hove. But we got on so nicely on the train that some instinct made me get out at Brighton, too. We lived close by the station, then, so he walked me home. The next day he came round in the afternoon and asked my mother if he could take me out for tea. Well, my mother, of course – she was very old fashioned – was very shocked. Someone I'd picked up on the train, she called him, and sent him packing. But he was on holiday down here, staying with his aunt, and he had nothing to do, so he came every day with the same request, but each time my mother sent him away. I was afraid he would give up. But then, luckily, my mother found out that his aunt was a very respectable old lady reputed to be worth a fortune. So at last she said yes, just for tea. Well, we didn't bother with tea, of course. We just walked for miles and miles, in the rain, all over Brighton. Then we walked all along the beach and got quite soaked, and it began to thunder. We sheltered under the pier for a while, and do you know what he said? He said: "Ethel Smith, I'm a penniless medical student and there's nothing I can give you, but I love you." Then it came on to rain even harder, and we decided we'd better make a dash for it. So we ran home. And then, of course, my mother scolded us, and what with all the flurry of drying our clothes and making hot drinks I never had a chance to tell him that I loved him too.'

Mrs Fox came to a standstill, and pointed towards the town.

'Funnily enough, although it's all changed now with all these new blocks of flats, I believe we could still take the short cut to my mother's house that Henry and I took that day. Shall we try?'

On the way there she told us she had heard the house had been a bed and breakfast place now for many years. But she would like to see the outside again.

It was a small, redbrick house between two creamy stone Regency houses. The only things it had in common with them was a bow window on the first floor, and a bed and breakfast sign on the front door. Joshua was enthusiastic to see inside, but Mrs Fox tried to restrain him.

'You know how unsympathetic landladies can be,' she protested. But he disentangled himself from her arm and rang the front-door bell. It was answered by a middle-aged woman with a bunch of dazzling blonde curls perched precariously on her head, stage make-up and a stained apron.

'I have a friend here,' said Joshua, dragging the reluctant Mrs Fox towards him, 'who lived in this house till just after the First World War. We've heard so much about it from her, we wondered if we could just glance at the inside?'

'Well, I don't mind if you do. There's no-one staying at the moment. Come on in.' She gave us a welcoming landlady smile and we followed her.

The room stretched from one end of the house to the other, a window at each end. Three different wallpapers covered the walls: one flowered, one geometrical and one covered with storks flying through pink clouds. Mrs Fox gasped, and dabbed at the flowers and cherry in her hat. She turned slowly round, taking in the lurex glitter of the curtains, the television on its spindly legs, the flight of paper angels left over from Christmas, above the modern brick fireplace with its electric fire, the leatherette three-piece-suite and the jumbo ashtray from Torquay.

'I bought it thirty years ago,' said blonde curls, 'and spent every penny I had doing the place up. It was a right shambles. Then only last year I did it right through again. Cost me a fortune, but it's worth it. I'm fully booked years ahead.'

Mrs Fox didn't seem to hear her. Suddenly, she smiled.

'You've certainly improved the place,' she said. 'I never could have imagined it so lovely and bright.' She struggled to take off her fur coat. I helped her. Its warm satin lining smelt faintly of her violet scent. 'It was always chilly, too, in spite of the coal fire. You've got it lovely and warm, haven't you?' Again she looked in some amazement round the sparkling room. 'When we lived here, this was two poky little rooms. Here, in this part, the front room, my father would play his violin on a Sunday afternoon. We weren't allowed near him. It was very dark, I remember, and filled with huge mahogany furniture which seemed to suck up all the light, and it always smelt musty. It seemed so much smaller.'

The landlady looked at her kindly and invited us to join her in a cup of tea. When she had gone out to the kitchen, Mrs Fox snapped back to the present.

'But still,' she said, thinking out loud, 'you should never go back. It's a silly thing to do. A silly thing to do.'

She sat down on one of the leatherette arm-chairs. It squeaked, and the embroidered antimacassar skidded sideways behind her head. Joshua and I stood in front of the electric fire, close but not touching. Mrs Fox looked up at us.

'We've had some good times,' she said. Joshua laughed. 'You'll have to meet Clare's husband,' he said. Mrs Fox sniffed.

'I'm not looking forward to that. It isn't that I'm not pleased that it's all worked out so well. It's just that I'm used to you two. We're all used to each other, aren't we?' She was unusually subdued. But then the landlady came back with a tray of tea, and switched on the lights. Mrs Fox slid forward on her chair.

'Edith would never have believed her eyes,' she smiled, and for some reason the rest of us laughed.

When we left the landlady Mrs Fox had one more request before we turned to London. She wanted to take a short walk on the beach.

The wind was colder now and the afternoon light had almost faded. Street lamps made pale holes in the sky, and the pier stuck out into the sea like a huge, dusky barn on stilts. As we walked along the front an old, shadowy man came towards us, distorted into strange shapes by the instruments that hung about him.

'You'd never believe it!' Mrs Fox cried out in delight, 'who would have expected such luck? A one-man band. I wonder if he would play for us?' She skipped up to him like a child and put a hand on his arm. She asked him to play.

'I'm on my way home, aren't I, lady?' he replied, nicely.

Mrs Fox pleaded with him further. Eventually, they struck up some kind of a bargain. Then while the musician tuned up – weird squeaks and thumps flew from his various instruments – Mrs Fox led Joshua and me down a flight of steps to the beach.

'He'll be some time,' she explained. 'Those things go out of tune as soon as you finish playing them.'

The tide was high. There was only a narrow strip of shingle along which we could walk. Mrs Fox pranced along the stones making them clatter and crunch in a kind of harmony with the small crashes from the breaking waves. She stopped, stooped down, and picked up a smooth white pebble. Fast and skilfully she curved back her arm, lunged forward and threw it with all her force. It made a brief white arc in the sky, then plummeted down into the dark sea.

'Did you see that? Did you see where it went? Not bad for my age, in a fur coat, is it? So out of practice, too.' She picked up another pebble. 'Henry and I would compete for hours. He was a marvellous pebble thrower, Henry.' She broke off to throw again. This time the pebble didn't go so far. 'Not such a good one. You have to choose your pebble carefully. You can blame a poor shot quite a bit on the pebble, you know.'

Joshua chose himself a flat white stone, and with less grace than Mrs Fox, hurled it into the water.

'Not bad! Not bad at all. But just you see, I can beat you.' She bent down again to look for another stone.

At that moment the musician on the pavement high above us stepped forward. A street lamp behind him threw his huge shadow down on to the beach, a bulging monster shape. With a nice sense of the dramatic, he raised his arms for a second, like a conductor, so that his shadow became a bird shape. Then the wings dropped and he began to play.

'When I'm Sixty-Four' thumped down upon us. *Bang clonk oink doom, clonk* ... Mrs Fox paused mid-throw to laugh.

'Cheeky!' she said. 'I'll show him I'm not in need of any looking after, am I?' and she thrust another pebble into the sea.

Joshua and I began to compete with her. Faster and faster we chose our stones and threw them with diminishing skill. The musician's shadow lapped over us, shrinking a little and swelling a little according to which instruments he played together. Joshua took my hand and whirled me round in a mad dance. Mrs Fox joined us. We skipped round in a circle, singing. The shingle slipped and scraped beneath our feet. On every fourth beat we paused, bent down, picked large stones and threw them, with one gesture, into the black chips of the waves. The wind, no longer cold, smelt of seaweed. A solitary gull cawed steeply up into the thick sky. We were confused with laughter.

When the tune came to an end, the dance came to an end. We clapped, but the noise was barely audible above the sea. Mrs Fox panted a little, and held her side. Joshua took her arm, suddenly concerned. She looked up at him, her face pale but excited.

'With a little more practice I wouldn't be surprised if you couldn't take on Henry one day,' she said. 'But I'm definitely not as good as I used to be. Give me a few days here, though, and I'd soon be up to my old standard.'

'I think we've done enough for one day, don't you?' Joshua let go of her arm. The musician began to play the march from *The Bridge on the River Kwai*.

'Just one more throw,' said Mrs Fox, 'to see if I can't beat you.'

Still panting, she stooped to choose another stone.

'This is a beauty. You couldn't find a better one on the whole beach.' It was flat, white, and almost perfectly round. She curved her arm again, tightened her mouth into a determined line, and threw. But this time it was feeble. The stone sank a few yards into the water. Mrs Fox sagged with disappointment.

'It's no good. Like Henry says, you should know when to stop.' Her hands fell to her sides. Her fingers plucked at bits of blue fur which straggled from her long sleeves. 'Well, perhaps we had better go.'

Joshua took her arm again and led her back towards the dark flight of steps. In slow motion they climbed the steps, in time with the music. On the pavement of the front again, now brilliant with lights, the wind seemed colder and fiercer. With a bare hand, her rings sparkling, Mrs Fox rammed her hat farther down on to her head.

'We must thank the man for his kindness,' she said. 'We must thank him for his splendid playing.'

Then, quite upright again, dignified and full of purpose, she marched towards him.

*

'D'you think I've remembered everything?'

'I think so.'

'All those new shirts?'

'Yes.'

'Plenty of socks?'

'Yes.'

'Pentels?'

'Yes.'

'You don't look after me badly, do you?'

Joshua was in the bath. Lying back, in the steam, not washing. I was on the three-legged cork stool.

'That was good, that chicken thing for dinner, wasn't it? We should have tried that place before.'

'Yes,' I said, 'we should.'

'We always meant to. You should have reminded me.' Pause. 'What are you thinking?'

'Nothing much.'

He offered me a soapy hand.

'Did you remember to get my sun lotion stuff?'

'Yes.'

'And a spare typewritter ribbon?'

'Yes.'

He grinned. Began to rub soap under one arm.

'You're marvellous, Face.'

'Oh, shut up.'

He grinned again and began under the other arm.

'Are you sure you're feeling all right now? I mean, your stomach and everything?'

'Yes, thank you. Fine.'

'You'll take care for a while, though, won't you? Thing like that takes a bit of getting over. Make Jonathan treat you carefully. Say you haven't been too well. Or are you going to tell him?'

'No.'

'What are you going to tell him about the last six months?'

'Nothing very much. I think it was part of our contract that we shouldn't make each other confess about whatever we'd been doing.'

'What do you think he's been up to?'

'I can't imagine. I expect he's been lonely. He's not

203

very good at being alone. Perhaps he really has been writing in his Roman attic.'

'Perhaps he's just about to have an epic novel published.'

'Perhaps.'

'So you'll be rich and famous.'

'Perhaps.'

'Will you ever want to see me again?'

'If you want. – Would you want to?'

'Not really. Small talk with Mr Lyall. "And perhaps you'd sign my copy for me, Jonathan old boy." You can imagine.'

'I suppose so.'

'Still, we might run into each other sometime, somewhere.'

'We might.'

'Not that we know many of the same people.'

'Well, just in the street.'

'Well, yes, we might, in the street.'

Joshua sat up, lifted a foot from the soap-misted water, and with intricate care began to wash each toe.

'Mrs Fox seemed tired this evening.'

'I think she overdid it.'

'Will you go on seeing her?'

'Of course. I'll probably go round to-morrow afternoon.'

'I'll send her lots of postcards. I wonder how she'll take to Jonathan?'

'Oh, she'll be won over by him in the end, I expect. He's got great charm.'

'So you've always said. But what else will you do?'

'When?'

'To-morrow.'

'Oh, to-morrow. To-morrow I'll finish packing up and tidying up here, then I'll go home and begin to get things ready for Tuesday.'

'For when Jonathan comes home?'

'Yes.'

Joshua dropped his first foot back in the water and picked up the other one.

'Well, you know my address in Mexico.'

'What do you mean?'

'You could send on anything I've forgotten.'

'Of course.'

'But I don't think I *have* forgotten anything, do you?'

'I don't think so.'

'All my new shirts?'

'We've been through all that.'

'So we have.'

He turned on the hot tap so that for a while we could not go on speaking. When the bath was full he lay back again, knees bent, hands tracing patterns under the water, an occasional finger surfacing to break a floating bubble of soap.

'D'you think it'll work?' he asked.

'Absolutely. I know it will.'

'Good. I always wanted you to go back, you know, all along.'

'Why?'

'Nothing to do with your not being the right person for me. Just because I always knew you believed implicitly in marriage, and that really you wanted it to work.'

'That's true,' I said. 'But that's not to say. . . .' Pause. This was my last chance to find out what I still didn't know. I would risk his anger. 'Was I ever all right for you?' I asked.

Joshua lifted a dripping arm and touched my chin with two fingers.

'Oh, Face,' he said, 'don't be silly.'

He stood up, then, and began to dry himself with a small black towel. I squeezed striped toothpaste for him on to his toothbrush.

'Do you remember?' Gaily I said it.

'For God's sake don't start remembering.' He rubbed the towel viciously over his face, then his hair.

'In fact, when I've gone, don't remember anything except that you once met a man called Joshua Heron, and by some measure of chance you and he were happy for a while. Will you do that for me, Face?'

'I will.'

'Good.' He opened the door so that the cold air from our bedroom blew upon us. He brushed his teeth, rinsed out the basin, turned out the light, got into bed and stretched out a hand for his schoolboy clock. With some difficulty, he set the alarm.

*

The next morning two members of the film crew picked him up early in a hired car. He didn't want me to go with them to the airport. He kissed me quickly and left in a rush. When he had gone, I searched the flat. For once, it seemed, he had remembered everything.

Chapter Fourteen

First, I opened the windows. The house smelt of polished furniture that has not been aired. Unlived-in. The woman who came twice a week had covered the sofa and armchairs in the sitting-room with dust sheets. She had arranged two piles of letters, one Jonathan's, one mine, on the desk. She had left me a note on the kitchen table. *I have taken the liberty of throwing away the piece of Stilton, it had gone mouldy.* Dated two months ago. It was the first time I had been in the house for three months, and that was only to collect more clothes. There was nothing in the fridge. Only two tins of soup in the larder.

Next, I had a bath. It was a pale blue bath. The wallpaper had matching pale blue roses. Jonathan liked blue. All his pyjamas were blue, with white initials on the pockets. He kept his pyjama tops on while he shaved in the mornings, while I was in the bath, but he took great care never to wet the collar. He hummed while he shaved. He was rather good at humming. Never out of tune. One Christmas I had found some blue after-shave lotion for his stocking. There was still a little at the bottom of the bottle on the shelf above the basin. I would get a new bottle, later to-day.

I dried in a huge navy towel, then walked naked into the bedroom. I sat on the kidney-shaped chintz stool in front of my dressing-table. The chintz seat felt cold for a moment. Half a dozen snapshots were stuck under the glass of the dressing-table. I studied them, tracing my finger on the cold glass round their frames: there was Jonathan with his arm round me in some Swiss mountain restaurant, a ski-ing holiday, our faces made harshly black and white by the flash bulb. We had drunk a lot of *gluwein* that night, and danced, and laughed. Enjoyed ourselves. There was Jonathan in his mother's rose garden, hands on hips, face screwed up against the sun; Jonathan sailing a small boat in Devon, slightly out of focus because of the choppy sea; Jonathan aged twelve, with smarmed-down choirboy hair, receiving a huge silver cup for swimming from a distinguished old woman in a velvet hat. There was one of me alone that Jonathan had taken with his Polaroid camera, a little faded. I sat on a rug in an indeterminate garden. I wore a cotton dress with a billowing skirt, and a cardigan. My hair was short and curled, and I smiled widely. It must have been a week or so after I first met Jonathan – perhaps the first weekend at his mother's house. I remember laughing at something he was saying while he took the photograph. He hadn't asked me to smile.

I looked at myself in the looking-glass. My face was much thinner, now. My hair much longer, straighter, straggly. It needed new highlights. There would be time, to-morrow. To-morrow in the morning. To-day I would shop, dust, clean, arrange roses. They would be expensive at this time of the year, but still. They were Jonathan's favourite flowers. He would hate to come back and find the house dusty, untidy and without flowers. It would have been so much easier if we could have met somewhere, caught a plane and flown away. Anywhere. Anywhere so long as it avoided all these preparations. But Jonathan expected preparations.

He would expect me to be ready for him, neat, in his favourite dress, the ice out – the ice tongs. I mustn't forget the ice tongs. Where were they? He would expect us to welcome each other home, and to forgive one another, and to make it all up over one gin and tonic. Or, knowing him, champagne. Well, we would. We would go on from there. I would heat up the veal escalopes cooked, as he had taught me, in cream sauce with brandy and mushrooms, and we would eat in the unused dining-room. Drink special wine. Candles. I must remember to get candles. By the end of dinner we would probably find ourselves laughing. In the past, it had always been easy to laugh together, in the end. If we could start laughing, if we could find something to laugh about, it would be all right. But which was his favourite dress?

I went to the cupboard. Everything hung limply. Thin, dim dresses they all seemed. Lifeless. They needed starch and ironing and air. They needed to be worn again. I took out a green dress covered with blue cornflowers. He liked that. I put it on. It was too long, drab. Side view, my bottom stuck out. My breasts sloped down and did something ugly to the front. I looked terrible. But perhaps with shoes, and a bra, and my hair done, to-morrow night, it wouldn't be so bad.

I took off the dress and hung it outside the cupboard to remind myself it needed ironing. I put on a pair of jeans and a shirt, and went downstairs, barefoot. Sat at the neat desk, found a piece of paper, and began to make a shopping list. *2 grapefruit pt. double cream roses veal sugar tonic water frozen peas coffee matches* – I could write with mechanical ease. I didn't have to think. The words appeared on the paper by themselves. *Hair lotion apricots soap candles I love you Jonathan Lyall I am your wife Clare Serena Lyall and this time it will be for ever more sempre toujours tomatoes salted peanuts and all the usual things like butter.*

All afternoon I shopped.

By the time I arrived home again it was too late to go and see Mrs Fox. I would go on Wednesday, perhaps even take Jonathan. She would be missing Joshua, I thought.

I dumped my shopping bags on the kitchen table and began to put things away. Very slowly, very methodically. Then I re-arranged the shelf of cookery books so that they were in order of height. The kitchen seemed to be paler green.

When there was nothing left to do in the kitchen I went back to the sitting-room. There, I re-arranged two more shelves of books. Five other shelves were filled with leather-bound volumes all the same height. I began to replace them so that the titles were in alphabetical order. But half-way through it seemed pointless, and I stopped.

I lit a cigarette, sat at the desk. Pulled open one of the drawers. It was neat with bundles of letters. Jonathan's writing, spidery and black. I pulled out one of the letters. It was written four years ago, from Manchester. He was up there seeing a man who had liked one of his plays.

My own darling, I read, *It's nice to be feeling as happy and as optimistic as I do at the moment about Screwball, but why does genius have to take one to God-forsaken places like Manchester? I miss you so much I can't tell you. I think of you all day and wonder what you're doing and I'm writing this because there's still another two hours until I can decently telephone you again. If the play is put on you will come up all the time, even for rehearsals, won't you? Just to say I love you, I love you, I love you, your silly old husband J.*

In those days he rang me every few hours if ever we

were forced to be apart, and wrote every day. I found the letter that told of Screwball's fate.

After all that waiting about, wasted days away from you, the beastly Mr Lewis said I was on the right lines but he saw no hope of actually putting the thing on. I could have cried. I needed you to be there to love and comfort me. Oh my darling, do you mind my constant failures? You say you don't, but I only half-believe you. I will stay till Monday when he says he will see me again – it just might be worthwhile. I do want to surprise you one day. Wait for me. The only thing I feel I'm good at is loving you. God knows what I'd do without you. Please don't ever leave me, darling. All love as ever your adoring husband J. P.S. I've bought an electric mixer in a cut-price shop.

I wound up both clocks. Checked the telephone to see it was working. Smoked several more cigarettes. Put the roses, expensive scentless buds, into a bucket of water.

Upstairs, I began to unpack my case. Slowly, again. I came to the box with the star-sapphire ring. Tried it on. Not strong enough light to force the star. I put it in a drawer under a pile of scarves. Then I found two notes from Joshua – the only notes he had ever written me.

Joshua Heron crept out because he didn't want to wake Funny Face. He doesn't apologise for not washing up his coffee cup and will be back at six to take various people to a theatre if they would like that.

The second one was written on the back of a restaurant bill, three months old.

Joshua Heron came back hopefully at lunchtime but found no-one. Would F.F. please ring J.H. as soon as she gets back to make up his mind about buying a corduroy jacket the colour of best quality hay?

I tore them up, into very small pieces, and threw them away. After that, I couldn't unpack any more. I left the rest of my clothes half in the case, half strewn about the floor. Then I went to bed. I had forgotten what a comfortable bed it was. At eight-thirty I turned out the light.

*

Four drum-majorettes skated across a huge rink towards me, holding up a striped canopy. Under the canopy, dressed in a dinner jacket, Jonathan skated in time with them. They stopped at the edge of the rink, in front of my seat. I rose, and moved the few paces towards them. As I did so, the huge audience, massed round the rink, began to applaud. Under the canopy I smiled at Jonathan and he gave me his hand. His fingers crackled and stung with ice. We began to skate away, looking for the exit to the wings. But it had disappeared. We skated round and round and the applause became louder. We kept passing Richard Storm, Mrs Fox and Joshua, sitting together in the front row. They had their arms intertwined, like people about to sing 'Auld Lang Syne'. They were laughing and laughing.

*

I woke at nine-thirty. I drew back the curtains and a cold grey light revealed the extent of the confusion on the floor: books, clothes, a pair of gum-boots still muddy from Norfolk. I would clear it all up, slowly, later. There were nine and a half hours to go.

I lay in the bath for a long time. After a while I thought I heard the creak of footsteps on the stairs. I listened again. Silence. Then a soft knock on the half-open door.

'May I come in?'

Ridiculously, I answered: 'Yes – who is it?'

Jonathan opened the door.

I stood up so fast the water swayed over the rdge of the

bath and onto the floor. It streamed down my stomach and thighs, and I felt myself crossing my arms over my breasts.

'Darling! Wait a minute. Here's a towel.' He held it in front of himself like a shield, and came towards me. We kissed, lightly, the towel still between us. Then I put my wet arms round his neck.

'Jonathan,' I said.

'Hurry up and get dry.' He seemed to stiffen a little, and moved away from me. I took the towel from him and stretched up to flip it over my shoulders. In the few seconds that I was naked to him his eyes flashed up and down my body. 'Heaven's, you're thin,' he said.

'So are you.' His hair, as well as his face, seemed thinner. I climbed out of the bath, sat on the edge, and began to dry. 'I thought you weren't coming till to-night,' I said. 'I'm afraid nothing's ready. It would have been, by to-night.'

'Well, there didn't seem much point in hanging around for another day, doing nothing, knowing you were back.' He sat on the lavatory, hitching up both legs of his trousers as he did so. It was a new suit, trim grey flannel. He fiddled with his navy silk tie. 'Do you mind?'

'Of course not. I'm just sorry I haven't got the house organised.'

'That doesn't seem very important.'

I raised my eyebrows.

'You look very brown,' I said, 'very well.'

'I am. I've had so much sun that I actually turned from lobster to brown. I bet you never imagined the day when that would happen.' He laughed and I smiled. He had a nice face.

'No,' I said. He folded his arms, leant back against the cistern and looked at me.

'How are you, darling?'

'I'm all right, too.'

'It's been a funny old six months.'

'Yes.' I was dry. 'I'm just going to put on some clothes. I won't be a moment.' He followed me into the bedroom.

'I'll go down and put on some coffee.'

'That's a good idea.' When he had gone I quickly made the bed. He might not want to wait until to-night.

By the time I went downstairs Jonathan was in the sitting-room, a tray of coffee set on the low table in front of the sofa. He had found the best cups, the ones I used when his mother came to tea. Suddenly I realised I was hungry and thirsty.

'How lovely,' I said. I sat beside him on the sofa. The chintz cushion crackled beneath me. 'Where's your luggage?'

'Still in the car.' He smelt of unfamiliar after-shave. Too sweet. He poured the coffee and hot milk, put in the sugar and stirred mine as well as his own.

'Well, well,' he said. 'Six months to the day. I heard from David you were well and happy.'

'I heard the same about you.'

'I think he quite enjoyed his self-appointed role of keeping us in touch. He doesn't change, David.'

'No, he doesn't.'

'He doesn't change.' He sat hunched up on the edge of the sofa, his knees wide apart, his hands clasped between them. 'Well, it's strange to be back.' He looked down at my hands. 'Where did you get that ring?'

'It belonged to Mrs Fox.'

'Who's she?'

I paused for a moment.

'Mrs Fox is an old woman I met. A friend. You must meet her.' I fingered the ring, imitating her gestures, the gestures I knew so well. Then: 'It's nice to have you back,' I said.

He turned to me, smiling.

'Look darling, you don't have to pretend. After these six months, we might as well be honest with one another.'

'What do you mean?'

'You know perfectly well what I mean.' He put a soft hand on my knee. 'Let me tell you something, Soo. Let me try to tell you something. That is: it's all right. You needn't worry any more. You needn't feel guilty any more, you know. I know what your decision is, and I want you to understand and believe me. *I don't mind*. I really don't, this time. No pretending. So long as you are happy, I'm happy for you. I mean that.'

'But darling, you've got it all wrong.' I put my hand on his. 'About my decision, I mean. What on earth made you think I wouldn't want you back? Why did you think I wouldn't want to come back to you?'

'I just assumed, from your behaviour before we parted. I hoped for a while you might change your mind. Then I heard you were happy with Joshua Heron. So I gave up hoping.' A long silence. Then:

'In that case, I've got a surprise for you,' I said.

'Oh?'

'It's all over with Joshua. There wasn't really any question of – anything permanent. He's gone to Mexico. I told him I was going back to you, and he was pleased.'

'You mean? – You want us to stay married? Is that what you mean?'

'Of course.' A look of something like fear crossed his face. He patted at his soft, sandy hair with a hand that shook a little, then bent his head and pressed his eyes into his palms.

'Oh Christ, my love,' he said quietly. 'Oh Christ, what a mess. What a bloody awful mess.'

'Why?'

'Why? Because it was true what I said earlier. Absolutely true. About my not minding about your not wanting me any more. You see, the thing is, I'm fixed up elsewhere, as it were.'

'You mean – ?'

'I've found somebody else.' He sat up then and took both my hands. Lowered his eyes. His eyelashes had gone very blond in the sun. 'I'm sorry, Soo.'

'Somebody else?' I said.

'Somebody else.'

'I see.' I tried to draw my hands away but he held them firmly.

'Don't run away from me.' I flopped back in the sofa. He let go of one hand to stroke my hair. 'I thought you'd be so pleased. I thought you'd be delighted when I told you I had booked an appointment with my solicitor this afternoon, and we would get divorced as soon as possible, and you could go back to Joshua. But what an irony of timing. What a cruel irony.'

'You want to marry her, then?' I asked.

'That's the plan.'

'Is she Italian?'

'No. She just lives in Rome. I think you met her once, actually. She says she remembers you, at a party you apparently went to with David. She's called Rose Maclaine.'

'The American? But I thought she and David – ?'

'They did. A rather one-sided little affair. David was

dotty about her. But she never pretended the feeling was mutual.'

'Then he introduced her to you?'

'Then he introduced her to me. And that was that. Very awkward for David and me, being such old friends, as you can imagine.'

'I imagine.'

'Still, it seems to be all right now. He's forgiven me. I took him out to dinner last night and he drank our health and said he hoped we would be happy.'

I smiled.

'Last week he rang me to say he hoped *we* would be happy.'

'He changes.' Pause. 'Oh Christ, Soo. What a mess. What are we going to do?'

'What do you want to do?'

'Don't sound like that. Here, let me kiss you. You're shaking.'

I let him kiss me. He kissed me on the eyes and the cheeks. Then he ran the hard point of his tongue round my closed lips, trying to make me smile. A trick he hadn't practised since before we married. But I didn't smile and he soon gave up.

'I can't very well fall out of love with Rosie and come back to you just because – '

'Of course not.'

'So what shall we do?'

'You had better go ahead with your plans.'

'How would you feel about that? I thought you were in love with Joshua, anyway? So it wouldn't matter to you very much, would it? I'm sure he'd have you back.'

'Don't worry about me.'

'Don't be silly, Soo. I do worry about you. I still care

217

about you, you fool. It's just that living with Rosie did the trick. It made me see all the things that were missing in our marriage. It made me realise that I was looking for something in you that didn't exist, and making do with all the things *you* thought I minded about. And it also dawned on me that I was absolutely the wrong man for you. I drove you mad, remember? I don't wonder, really, when I think back on it.'

'You've got it all nicely worked out.'

'Oh, my love. Forgive me.'

'There's nothing to forgive. Does Rosie make you happy?'

'Very. She's a marvellous girl. So – organised.' He looked suddenly hopeful. 'Do you think we could all be friends?'

'I expect we probably could.'

'Are you going to make a fight for me? Try to get me back?'

'I don't see any point, if you want to go.'

'Quite.' He smiled again. 'The trouble with you, darling, is that you're so bloody reasonable you'd drive any man to despair. Let me give you one bit of advice. If ever you fall in love with anyone again, be unreasonable.' He stood up and hitched up his trousers. 'You've taken so much trouble. Those lovely roses, and I saw there was veal in the fridge. It could have been a marvellous homecoming.'

'Don't put off your solicitor,' I said. 'And you might recommend one to me.'

'Are you sure? I'm sorry, darling.' He paused. 'As a matter of fact, what I had planned to do was to fly back to Rome to-night and settle a few things over there, then come back again next week. But I could go later.'

'No. Go to-night. You might as well.' I stood up and picked up the tray. He took it from me. 'How's the writing?' I asked.

'Going rather well, actually. I'm working on a little play called Back to Front. Rosie's keen to play the lead, so we're going to try to organise that. I showed part of it to David, and he's really enthusiastic. He says he knows a new young manager who might like it.' He smiled wryly. 'So nothing's changed.'

'No,' I said. 'I hope it gets put on.'

We went into the kitchen. A light rain sprayed against the window.

'Bloody English weather,' said Jonathan. 'It looks nice in here, though, darling. I always thought this kitchen was my *pièce de résistance*, didn't I?'

'Yes.'

'You can keep the house if you like. I mean, I don't want any of my money back.'

'You're very generous. Thank you.'

'And you can cite Rosie, of course.'

'All right, if that's easiest.'

'But we could talk about all those sort of arrangements when I get back next week. I don't really feel much like going into them now. I mean, I'm bloody happy and all that, I really am. But it's always nasty, having to make the actual break.'

'Quite.' He came and stood very near me. There was a long thin scratch on his chin where he had cut himself shaving. It was covered by a delicate scab of barely dried blood.

'You must think I'm a terrible shit,' he said.

'Oh no. It was my fault just as much as yours. More, probably.'

'But I don't think, feeling like I do about Rosie, and you feeling like I suppose you do about Joshua, that there's any point in our trying to make a go of it any more, do you?'

'Absolutely not.'

'Besides, six months apart kills a lot of things.' He kissed me on the cheek again. 'Oh darling. What a confounded mess. I think I'm going to cry.'

'Don't do that.'

'Well, there's not much point in my hanging around any more, is there? It'll only upset both of us. I'll call you next week.'

'I'll be here.'

'Will you be all right?'

'Of course.'

'I don't think you really mind.' He took the clean white handkerchief from his breast pocket and blew his nose very loudly. 'What fools we are.' We went to the front door. 'You must put on some weight,' he said. 'You're too thin.'

Outside, his old blue Vauxhall was covered with a million drops of rain that weren't heavy enough to run down. A leopard printed scarf lay on the back seat.

'Bloody English weather,' Jonathan said again. 'Always the same in this country.' He squeezed my hand. 'Well, darling, I'll be off, then.'

'See you next week.' We kissed each other on the cheek once more.

'I was so convinced you wouldn't want me. Funny how wrong you can be, even about someone you've been married to for six years.'

'Go on,' I said, 'I'm getting wet.'

He got into the car and started the engine. Its muffled rumble was horribly familiar. Jonathan's thumbs met at the top of the steering wheel. He had often said he thought it was the most comfortable way to drive. He raised one hand to wave. I waved back. The car drew slowly away. Puddles spluttered beneath the wheels for a moment, then were still again. I shut the front door.

*

It was definitely cold in the sitting-room now. I sat on the sofa again and wondered how to get warm. I had forgotten to ask Jonathan to turn on the central heating.

I blew on my hands. The crayon drawing of Richard Storm smiled down at me. Later, I would take it down. Jonathan smiled from a silver frame, too. It was his favourite picture of himself, taken when he was in the Coldstream Guards by a Bond Street photographer who had touched up his pale eyebrows. I would take that down as well.

I thought how I had felt quite proud when Jonathan had walked into the bathroom this morning. He had looked so agreeable. I was pleased he was back.

I wondered what to do with the veal and the roses.

I listened to the clocks ticking, sometimes together, sometimes one just a little ahead of the other.

I don't know how long I sat there.

But after a while I went to the kitchen and turned on the cold tap. The water pattered on to the zinc bottom of the sink, louder as I turned the tap faster. I held my hands so that the fingers drooped under the cascade of water. It was so cold, they soon felt quite numb. I turned the tap off with the palm of my hand.

A walk, I thought. If I walked fast I would get warm.

I put on my mackintosh and left the house, slamming the door behind me.

It was raining harder now. I walked carelessly, not bothering to avoid the puddles, so that water splashed up my legs. Soon my hair was soaked and drips kept on running into my eyes.

It took about half an hour to get to Mrs Fox. Surprisingly, the downstairs front door was ajar. I pushed it open and went in. The landlady was coming downstairs, her huge slack breasts rolling about under a pink jersey.

'Oh, it's you,' she said. 'Another of her friends.' She slapped the banisters with a fat hand and heaved herself down the last few steps.

'Is she in?' I asked.

'No dear, she's out. Out for good. Didn't you know?'

'Know what?'

'Oh, I see. You didn't know.' She lowered her voice. 'Mrs Fox passed away Sunday night, they reckon.'

'She's dead?' I said. The landlady's eyes hardened with power.

'Dead as a doornail, dear. Heart attack. She might have been there for days if yours truly hadn't noticed her milk still outside her door yesterday dinner time. She always took her milk in, regular. So I thought, I thought to myself: my, something funny's up. I banged on the door, noisy as you like, but not a cheep. So I phoned the police. They come up, of course, and break the lock. They found her on the bed. Hat still on and all.'

I leant against the wall. A bit of plaster crumbled behind my shoulder and fell to the stone floor. The landlady's face erupted into a huge sun of crumbling white flesh that sprouted from the grey stone stairs rising behind her.

'Where is she?' I asked.

'They took her away, ambulance men, not long after. They asked me if I knew any of her relations. Course, I couldn't help them.'

'Where did they take her to?'

'Blow me if I didn't ask. Fulham, I should imagine. The hospital.' More plaster broke and fell away from the wall behind my shoulder. 'Careful,' she said, 'that wall's coming down.'

'So it is,' I said. The landlady opened the front door. She looked at the rain, diminished to a drizzle now.

'Ooh, it isn't half coming down cats and dogs, isn't it? Well, I must be getting back to work. See that other man shuts the door behind him when he leaves, will you? You know what men are.'

'What man?'

'There's another of her friends upstairs. Don't know for the life of me what he expects to find, poking about up there. The door's locked, but he asked me to leave him on his own – I don't know.'

She went out, shutting the front door. I went to the well of the staircase, held on to the banisters and looked up at the regular flights of stairs. Quietly, a man was coming down from the top, his footfall clacking gently on the stone. As he came nearer I saw that it was Cedric Plummer. The man from the R.S.P.C.A.

'Hello,' he said, as he saw me.

'Hello.'

He came down the last flight, leaning heavily on the banisters. He wasn't wearing his uniform, but the dark suit and plum tie he had worn at Mrs Fox's party.

When he reached the bottom he stopped beside me. We stood looking at each other in the dim light of the drab hallway. There were rims of yellow crust at the roots of his eyelashes. The eyelids themselves were red and puffy.

'The landlady told me she was dead,' I said.

Mr Plummer shrugged his shoulders, unclenched his hands, and held them up like two heavy white flags.

'Who could conceive such sadness?' he replied. 'Who could conceive such sadness?' He moved away from me, towards the front door. 'I'd just come up to take her home to us for the day. She had always wanted to see Epsom. Nancy had baked her special sponge cake, and we had the place all looking spick and span.' He paused. 'She always said she wanted to see Epsom, Mrs Fox did, you know.' He paused again. 'To think, she never saw it.'

He turned his face quickly from me, pulled the door open, and went down the steps.

Alone in the hall I listened to the silence. For the first time, no music came from the top floor. The Japanese mobile that hung from the naked light bulb swung a little in the draught, faintly patterning the dingy walls.

It was cold and damp. Rain from my wet hair ran down the inside of my mackintosh collar.

I went on holding the clammy banisters, until a moment of dizziness passed, and then I followed Mr Plummer through the front door.

Outside, the rain had almost stopped. The sky was brightening. I began to run in the direction of Fulham. Somehow, I had to find a brass band.